PLOT TWIST

PLOT TWIST

DONNA J. THOMPSON

ReadersMagnet, LLC

TABLE OF CONTENTS

Chapter 1..1

Chapter 2..14

Chapter 3..22

Chapter 4..32

Chapter 5..38

Chapter 6..48

Chapter 7..62

Chapter 8..70

Chapter 9..77

Chapter 10..84

Chapter 11..92

Chapter 12..99

Chapter 13..114

Chapter 14..119

Chapter 15..126

Chapter 16..141

Chapter 17..151

Chapter 18..155

Chapter 19..161

Chapter 20..168

Chapter 21..177

Chapter 22..186

Chapter 23..195

Chapter 24..201

In memory of my grandmother, Eliza Frances Ross Jackson, who always had faith that I would become a published writer. I know she is looking down and smiling.

I would like to acknowledge my granddaughter, Cassie Thompson, whose name I used for one of my main characters in my book. I want her to see proof that dreams really can come true.

CHAPTER 1

---◆---

Karl Larkin, lead detective for the Springfield Police Department, says murder is like having a tooth pulled. No one wants to do it, but sometimes it is necessary, or so the murderer thinks. Unfortunately, in the twenty-odd years he has worked as a police officer, he has seen plenty of extractions.

His parents dreamed of sending their only son to college to become a doctor, or better still a lawyer, but Larkin had other plans. Right out of high school, while they were trying to decide which Ivy League school he should attend, Larkin enrolled in the police academy.

It had caused a breach in the family, but the man marched to the beat of his own drum, and he knew that being a detective would make him happy.

He had a nose for it, his colleagues said, and sometimes he stuck his nose where others thought it didn't belong. It had earned him the nickname of Columbo, given to him by his fellow police officers, because of his unusual ability to home in on a guilty suspect and stay with them until they either confessed or committed suicide. He had that in common with the TV personality, but the likeness ended there.

Columbo always looked as though he had crawled out of bed, and dressed in the dark, where Larkin looked manicured with every hair in place. He was a health nut. He prepared his own lunch, while the others sent out for a greasy burger, or pizza. Instead of hitting the couch with a bag of potato chips and a six-pack of beer as soon as he left work, he headed for the gym.

That morning started like most at the 19th Precinct, all hustle and bustle of men rushing to balance home life with their jobs.

Larkin sat at his desk watching the activity through the glass doors of his office. In front of him sat his only vice, a large steaming cup of coffee with one spoon of creamer. The cup, a gag gift from his staff, said, "The nose knows."

Cramer entered carrying a large box of doughnuts. He was thirty-something, chunky, and on his way to becoming a fat man. He had a likeable personality, which made him easy to work with, and if the office-mill gossip was right, Larkin was personally mentoring him to be his number one assistant. In all truthfulness, Larkin couldn't see him being the next Sherlock Holmes, but he did have the one thing Larkin recognized, the love for his job. They also worked well together, proving opposites do attract.

"Want a roll?" Cramer asked the same question every morning.

"Why do you do that?" his boss asked as the younger man heaved his husky frame upon the corner of his desk.

"Do what?"

"Ask me if I want one of those artery-clogging morsels of pretty poison."

"You make them sound so appetizing." Cramer smacked his lips and tried talking around the piece in his mouth. "It won't hurt to have one every now and then."

Larkin made his point by poking him as if he were the Pillsbury Dough Boy. "It hasn't hurt you, has it?"

"It's better than the caffeine you hype yourself up on." Cramer opened a pint of milk and drank it straight from the carton.

Larkin winced, for the crack about caffeine had hit home. He had tried to give it up, but it was an addiction. He didn't smoke, or drink, but he did crave a hot cup of coffee.

"I don't know why you stay so buff, ain't a woman that would have you." Cramer carried on with his good-natured banter, smacking his lips and licking the sugar off his fingers.

Larkin shook his head, and thought, *It's about time for the phone to ring, and he'll surely get slobber all over the receiver.* Sure enough, the phone rang.

"Homicide-Larkin's office. What can I do for you?" Cramer licked his fingers and wiped them on his pants. He was frowning as he listened to the other party. "I see-we'll be right there."

"What's up?" The grave look on Cramer's face said he wasn't going to be enjoying the rest of his coffee.

"They need us out on Pitchin Road. You know the Cromwell Estate."

Everyone in town knew Lawrence Cromwell, a noted plastic surgeon. A huge brick wall with closed gates surrounded his place. Larkin had been by it, but never dreamed he would be inside.

The caller had been Mrs. White, who introduced herself as the cook. Her details were sketchy, but she was certain of two things. Mrs. Cromwell had disappeared, and Mr. Cromwell had found a note saying kidnappers had his wife.

"Why did they call us?" Larkin asked.

"It seemed that our famous district attorney, Howard Deets, is a friend of Cromwell's. Instead of calling the police, Cromwell called his old buddy."

"That doesn't explain why homicide was called in."

"A patrolman found her car with a substantial amount of blood ..."

"Oh," Larkin exhaled. It had been awhile since there had been more than the drug-related deaths, or a drive-by shooting the department had to deal with. A few domestic violence cases had ended in murder, but they solved themselves when the spouse confessed. Somehow, he knew that this was going to be a long one. He felt it in his gut.

The two detectives sat at the front gates wondering how to get in when they mysteriously slid open. Cramer jumped at the sound and no more had he pulled inside when they slid closed behind them.

"Nice and secluded back here," Larkin commented on the tree-lined lane.

"Damn spooky, if you ask me." Cramer shivered as he drove toward the front of the mansion.

Larkin had to agree, but didn't voice his opinion. He was too busy taking in his surroundings.

An elderly butler let them into the main hall and showed them to the drawing room, where the anxious family sat waiting.

Larkin recognized Cromwell from his TV commercials touting him to be the best plastic surgeon of all time. As the lead detective and his fellow officer entered the room, Cromwell came to them with an outstretched hand. Both officers shook hands and introduced themselves, and Cromwell asked them to take a seat.

Cramer obliged, taking a chair over to the side, but Larkin declined. "I'd prefer to stand, if you don't mind. I find I think much better standing. My assistant needs to sit because he will be taking a few notes."

"Of course, if that is what you prefer," Cromwell agreed. "Can I offer you something to drink? Perhaps a cup of tea or coffee."

Larkin fought the urge to say yes to the coffee. Cramer also turned it down. There was an unspoken law about not being distracted by food or drink while working with Larkin.

"I'd like to get started if you don't mind." Larkin's eyes took in the people who sat in a circle as if they had been positioned. He walked over and leaned against a curio cabinet, and for some reason thought of the bungling police detective in the movies.

Maybe it was because of the stares from a beautiful woman who was eyeing him curiously, sizing him up. It was about time for the cabinet to overturn and the figurines to break into a million pieces. He stood away from the cabinet. The woman smiled as if reading his mind.

"This is my daughter, from a previous marriage, Cassie Thompson."

Larkin judged her about thirty-five to forty. Her light brown hair caressed the top of her shoulders, and as she moved her slim figure advertised perfection. What made her so attractive was the way her eyes twinkled in amusement as she watched how uncomfortable her stare was making him. He could have kicked his own rear for acting like a schoolboy.

"Ms. Thompson," Larkin acknowledged. "Do you live here?"

"Heavens no," Cromwell answered for her. "My daughter has a townhouse on the east side of Springfield."

She said nothing, but the twinkle was still in her eyes and a smile played around the fullness of her lips. *Maybe the woman couldn't talk,* Larkin thought.

Her father moved on. "This is my daughter Tina; she is sixteen." The girl was sullen, her eyes red from crying. She didn't speak at the introduction. Her dark hair was spiked, and she wore a ring in her left brow. She looked like a handful to Larkin, who didn't envy Cromwell, having to raise her for the next few years.

"This is my son, Todd. He is nineteen." Cromwell sounded bored, or maybe less than proud of the boy. "Todd doesn't think I handled the situation... correctly."

"I just think you should have called the police sooner," Todd snapped.

Tina said nothing, but her eyes agreed with her brother.

"Look, everyone's nerves are on edge. Let's let the police decide what we need to do from this point on." The woman could talk, and she had a lovely voice.

"Is this the whole family?" Cramer asked.

"We're waiting for Julie's sister and her family to arrive," Cromwell said. "I called her and her husband an hour ago. They should be here any time." He consulted his watch.

"Is Julie your wife?"

Cromwell looked up at Cramer. "I'm sorry. Yes, Julie is my wife."

"What's the sister's name?"

"Carrie Risner is my sister-in-law's name, and her husband is James.

"Their eighteen-year-old son, Toby, graduated ahead of schedule. He's even been accepted by Yale," Cromwell seemed to be making a point of letting everyone know how proud he was of his nephew.

"Are you going to be a Yale man?" Larkin directed his question to Todd.

The boy never answered, only hung his head, causing Larkin to regret asking.

"I'm afraid that my son will be lucky to make it through high school, Mr. Larkin," Cromwell sniffed.

"Sounds sort of like me," Larkin offered. I didn't drop out of school, but I am a disappointment to my folks. They wanted me to be a lawyer; instead I became a cop." Larkin hoped he had made up for putting the boy on the spot. He darted a quick look at Cassie. There seemed to be a growing respect in her eyes. She was aware of what he had tried to do.

"When did you first realize your wife was missing, Mr. Cromwell?"

It amazed Cramer, how Larkin could be having a casual conversation, and, all at once, come out with something relevant to the case. He had seen suspects blurt out something incriminating before they had time to think.

"We had a fight Friday evening."

"Here at the house?"

"No-no." Cromwell looked embarrassed. "She came by the office just before closing time. My secretary and I were having coffee together. It had been a long hard day and we were trying to relax before going home. We were laughing when Julie came storming in, misunderstanding what was going on, and caused quite a scene."

"Was there something going on?"

Suddenly Cromwell sounded tired. "I'm afraid my wife is a very jealous woman, Mr. Larkin. She's suspicious of every woman I meet."

"You said your secretary and you were amused about something?"

"A patient of mine wanted a breast augmentation. Terry, my secretary, made a humorous comment about it."

"Are you in the habit of discussing your patients with your employees, Doctor?"

Cramer could see Cromwell's jaws tighten as he spoke. "As a rule I do not, but Terry asked me what the woman wanted done and when I told her, she said, 'My God, the woman will fall on her face. You see-the woman has ample breasts already."

"So your wife came in and upon seeing you two laughing together, misconstrued the events and caused a scene. Is that right?"

"You shouldn't do things like that," Tina snapped. "You know how paranoid she gets."

"Honey," his voice softened as he spoke to his young daughter. "I didn't know she was there."

"You were kind of distracted," his daughter accused.

"You were there?" Larkin addressed the girl.

"Yes, my mom wanted a witness. She is convinced there is something going on between Dad and his secretary."

"I see."

"Ahem," Cassie cleared her throat, as if hoping to defuse the tension.

"So you had a fight," Larkin wanted to get back on track. "Then what happened?"

"After Julie and Tina left, I apologized to Terry for the things my wife had said."

"What kind of things were said?"

"She cursed her, and yelled obscenities. I knew that, if I went home, I would have to listen to more of the same in front of the children. I just wasn't up to that."

"So you tried to soothe your secretary, and not your wife."

"I knew it would do no good ... "

"Excuse me, Mr. Cromwell, but it seems to me the most natural thing would be to try to calm your wife."

"You wouldn't understand. You're not family," Cromwell said shaking his head.

"No, I don't understand. I mean, your wife is upset, and it looks like the normal thing would be to go after her ..."

"Dad, why don't you just tell him the way it is," Cassie could take it no longer. "The woman couldn't be reasoned with."

"So, she is difficult?"

"No, she is impossible."

"He's not the easiest person to live with," Todd broke in.

"Let's move on," Larkin said. He didn't want this to get out of hand. It accomplished nothing when families started choosing sides, but it could get ugly. "What happened then?"

"I told you. I knew if I went home, she would be ranting and raving in front of the children. I had had a bad day, and I didn't feel like dealing with her, so I went to a bar. I drank until about one o'clock. I knew I was too drunk to drive, so I called Cassie to take me home. I got home around one-thirty, I guess."

"Was your wife at home?"

"No, she wasn't."

"Why didn't you call the police at that time?"

"I noticed that none of her clothes were missing, and her car was gone. I figured she would be back once she cooled off. I was tired so I undressed and went to bed."

"Let me get this straight. Your wife is missing, you had just had a huge fight, and you just calmly went to bed."

"Mr. Larkin, you don't know the situation. You wouldn't understand ..."

"Cassie, it's okay. Just leave it alone." Cromwell intervened before she could say any more. It was easy to see that she was defensive when it came to her father.

"Did she come home Saturday?"

"No."

"Did you hear from her?"

"No."

"But you still didn't call the police."

"I told you I figured it would take a few days for her to cool off." He raked his fingers nervously through his graying hair.

"Did you hear from her Sunday?"

"That is when I found the note."

"The ransom note?"

"I had gotten up late. It was about eleven o'clock and I usually get up around six. I had a bowl of cereal and started outside to get the paper. I looked down and there lay the envelope in the middle of the entrance hall. I thought it was probably from Julie so I tore it open and began to read. It was from the kidnapper."

"Do you have the note?"

"Yes, I have it here in my pocket." He took it out and handed it to Larkin.

The note was words cut from the newspaper or a book and pasted onto white bond paper. Larkin slipped on rubber gloves before taking the folded piece of paper.

It said:

We have your wife. We want one million dollars in small unmarked bills. Divide the money and put each half in identical carrying bags. Take the money down to the boat docks of Buck Creek Lake, Tuesday morning at 2:00 AM. Make sure you are there on time. After closing time, the management blocks the entrance with a chain. Leave your car and walk the rest of the way. This way we can tell if you came alone. Find a boat named Sea Angel and place both bags of money underneath the tarp covering it. Get back in your car and drive home. We will release your wife within the hour. If you don't follow the orders exactly, or if you involve the police, we will kill her.

Larkin slipped the note into a plastic envelope, and put it in his pocket. "I'll have the forensic people try to get prints, but I doubt it will do any good. Has anyone handled it except you?"

"No, I showed it to no one. I didn't want to upset the other children, so I called Cassie. We both felt I didn't dare go to the police, for the kidnappers could be watching me. I decided to do what they ask..."

Larkin could tell there was a close bond between the woman and her father, and it was only natural, after a shock, to go to someone you trust. Another set of prints on the note would have complicated matters, so he was glad that Cromwell hadn't shown it to anyone else.

"So, you talked it over with your daughter, and you both agreed?"

"We felt we had no choice but to comply."

"So you did what?"

"I went home and called John Tremor, he's a friend of mine, who is president of Huntington Bank. He was on the golf course, but his wife gave him my message and he called me back around noon. I told him what I needed, and he had a million questions. He wasn't sure if he could get me the money that fast. I finally had to tell him what was going on. He said he would start the process the first thing Monday morning and would have the money by the end of the day. He told me not to worry. They would get as much as they could from the bank and he would get the rest from his safe if he had to. He knows I'm good for it; I guess there is just a lot of hassle because of the paperwork and stuff." Larkin nodded his head and he continued. "I hung up the phone and paced the floor the rest of the day. About six o'clock the phone rang. I thought it might be the kidnappers, but it was Cassie, calling to see how I was doing. She said to let her in, that she was on her way over to keep me company."

"So Ms. Thompson came to the house Sunday night?"

Lawrence nodded his head. "She has been here ever since."

"Where were the other two children?"

9

They both slept in till noon or after. Tina wanted to go to a friend's house and Todd wanted to go out also. I had to tell them what was going on."

"Were the kids upset?"

"Of course they were upset," Cromwell barked.

"Let's go back to the note. You said it was on the floor, in front of the mail slot?"

"It was."

"How did this person get in? Aren't the front gates locked?"

Cromwell thought for a second. "Yes, we keep the gates locked. I have no idea how they got in."

"Could it have been someone in the house?"

"What are you implying?" Cromwell bristled.

"I'm simply trying to get the facts. If the gates were closed, how did an intruder deliver the note?"

"1 have nobody new working for me, and I would trust my employees with my life."

"Would you trust the same people with your wife's?"

Cassie looked at the inspector with a stare that was less than flattering. It was easy to see she didn't like this line of questioning.

"I don't believe that my staff is involved with this."

" 1 didn't say they were."

The accusation was dawning on Lawrence. Larkin believed it was one of them.

"I don' t like what you' re implying, Detective."

"Excuse me, Mr. Cromwell, but your wife has been missing since Friday. It is now Tuesday and you're just now involving the police. You said you found a note in the floor, presumably put through the mail slot. This person was able to get through locked gates, and you're telling me no one who lives here or works here is involved. Something doesn't add up."

"I know- it doesn't make sense, but that is what happened."

"Let's get back to the story. What happened next?"

"Tremor and I agreed to meet at the bank on Monday before it opened. I took two identical bags with me. Tremor had the money ready. We divided it like the note said and I left."

"How did he come up with that much money before the bank opened?"

"He knows a lot of rich people who owe him favors."

"So, you know people who have this kind of money just lying around?"

"I have quite a bit here as well."

"I wouldn't say that out loud," Cramer warned. "Someone might want the rest of it."

"Look, Mr. Larkin. The money doesn't matter. I just want my wife back." Cromwell seemed to age before their eyes. Larkin almost believed it was true.

"So now you have the money. What did you do next?"

"I hurried back home hoping the kidnappers might call and we could set up an earlier time to deliver the money. They hadn't called, so we sat around on pins and needles just waiting until time to go to the lake."

"That must have been rough?"

"You'll never know."

"So you took the money and put it on the boat like you were supposed to?"

"You should have called the police earlier," Todd interjected.

"I told you they were going to kill her if I contacted the police," Cromwell hissed.

Larkin shook his head. Didn't the crazy man understand that they probably killed her anyway? "So you delivered the money?"

"Yes, then I drove home and waited for them to release her. I waited an extra hour, figuring she would need time to get home. When I realized they probably weren't going to let her go, I called Deets."

"What time was that?"

"It was exactly four o'clock this morning."

"I wonder why he waited so long to call us," Larkin thought aloud.

"I'm afraid I'm to blame for that," Cromwell admitted. "I didn't want the press to get wind of this, so I asked him to send out a few policemen to look for her car. I hoped she would be found and this cleared up before the media found out."

"And Deets agreed?"

"He's a good friend."

Larkin knew that Deets was a good friend to anyone who had money and influence, but didn't bother saying so to Cromwell. The man was already aggravated with him for the line his questioning had taken. If there was one thing the detective knew, it was that you could catch more flies with honey than with vinegar. He would try to be nicer.

"Someone said they found her car."

"Yes-an officer was looking around the lake, because that is where I told Deets I delivered the money. They found her vehicle behind the building that sells fishing licenses and boat tags. There was blood in it."

Tina gasped. It must have been the first time the girl had heard this news.

Todd turned a deadly pale, telling Larkin that he hadn't known either.

Cassie showed no emotion. Larkin couldn't tell if she had been privy to the information or not.

"Deets had Mrs. White call you after they found her car. He said you were the best."

Larkin found that hard to believe, for he and Deets had more than a few run-ins because of the way he handled his investigations. He let that pass and went on. He looked toward Cramer, who raised his eyes. He could tell that Cramer found it hard to believe as well.

"Did the policeman who found her car say there appeared to have been a struggle?"

"Yes, the officer told Deets that it looked as though she fought her attacker."

"Where is the automobile now?"

"It was taken to the impound lot is all I know."

"Good. The forensic people will be going over it by now."

"Will they keep me informed of what they find?"

"They will let me know and I will keep you abreast of developments. Do you have your cell phone with you?" he directed the question to Cramer.

Cramer held it up, to show him. He believed in his phone, he always carried it.

"Call forensics and ask them to get out here."

"Is that necessary?" Cromwell had come to his feet. "There is nothing here they need to see." He was angry that Larkin would even suggest such a thing.

"We need to dust for fingerprints. Maybe our delivery boy left some evidence. I also need a hairbrush belonging to your wife." Seeing the look on Cromwell's face he explained, "We have to make sure the blood in your wife's car is hers."

"Damn," Cromwell exclaimed. "Who else's could it be?"

"The person she fought with."

Tina headed off to get the brush after Cassie made eye contact with her and nodded her head.

"We will also need a DNA sample from everyone in the family." This really threw Cromwell into a tailspin. "Why in the name of heaven are you putting the family through this? None of us have anything to do with this."

"Because we need to eliminate all of you. I don't want a lawyer getting up in court and saying we aren't able to prove it's your wife's blood. That it could belong to another member of the family that had an accident in her car. Deets will tell you, Mr. Cromwell; I like to cover all bases."

"If it's necessary, the family will be happy to give you a sample," Cromwell agreed. He looked from one to the other of the assembled group.

CHAPTER 2

---◆---

J ust then, the doorbell sounded, and with a flurry of activity, loud voices were coming toward them.

The woman was in her mid-forties, dark hair, and extremely thin. She went to Cromwell and embraced him. The man was tall and wore the dark weathered look of someone who spent a good deal of time in the sun. He followed the woman as if he was used to doing so.

Cromwell introduced the couple as his sister-in-law, Carrie Risner, and her husband, James.

"Where is Toby?" Cromwell asked.

"He went on to school. I haven't told him about this yet. I was hoping it might be cleared up before I had to."

It was amazing how people believed the police could work miracles, Larkin thought. Maybe the woman was an extreme optimist, or better still, maybe she knew something they didn't.

"Is there a reason you thought it might be cleared up by now?" Larkin studied her intently as she began to speak.

"Mr. Larkin, is it?" She turned her attention to him. "I'm sure you will soon find that my sister has a flair for the dramatic."

"What are you implying, Mrs. Risner? That your sister may have set this up herself?"

Lawrence Cromwell frowned at his sister-in-law as though he resented her for bringing it up. He was nervously raking his fingers through his hair as he always did when he was agitated.

"My wife has left a couple of times before," he admitted.

"Lawrence, you know she's capable of staging the whole thing herself, and it's been a lot more than two or three times that she's left you. Let's be honest here."

"This time is different, Carrie. They found her car with blood in it."

Shock washed over her face. "I'm sorry, Lawrence. I didn't know."

James Risner sat very quietly looking from one to the other as they spoke. Larkin wondered what was going on in his mind.

"What's your take on all of this, Mr. Risner?"

"All I know is what I've been told." He let the detective know that he was staying out of it if he could.

"Where do you folks live?"

"We live about seven miles from here, in the country," Carrie said. "Why?"

"Could I have your address?" Larkin asked. "We may have questions later."

Carrie looked apprehensive, but told her husband to give it to Cramer, who was writing furiously.

"I will also need your address," he told Cassie, "and your phone number." Then as an afterthought he told Cramer, "Get Risner's number also." It wouldn't look good if he only asked for Cassie's.

Just when it was getting interesting, the forensic people invaded the place. Larkin pulled David Blake aside and told him what he wanted.

The leader of the science department didn't take crap from anybody. He was huge, but not fat; and the mere size of the man was intimidating. He took a swab of the inside of the mouth of everyone present, and his assistant bagged and labeled it. Larkin was glad the Risners had shown up in time to be a part of it.

The process upset Carrie Risner, but her husband seemed resigned to the fact. The kids acted bored, and Cassie just wanted it over with and everyone out.

"We will also need your son's DNA"

"Lawrence, do something. How dare they treat us all like criminals?"

"We need to eliminate everyone we can, Mrs. Risner. I feel that the perpetrator had to be familiar with the house and grounds. I noticed that the envelope that held the ransom note wasn't self-sealing. The perpetrator probably licked it. If it isn't your son's DNA on the flap, then he's in the clear."

"I just don't see why this is all necessary." She threatened, "I'll get a lawyer."

"You could do that, but the DA is a friend of Mr. Cromwell's and he is very interested in the case. He will just have a judge override you."

She turned a beet red; Larkin could tell she was furious. "I don't like my son being exposed to this. And I don't like to be threatened, Mr. Larkin," she hissed.

"Mrs. Risner, I am working on a case and I will do what I have to do."

"Carrie," Cromwell spoke directly to his sister-in-law, "we have all given a sample. Please just cooperate with the detective." His eyes pleaded with her.

Larkin watched her soften. The woman had feelings for Cromwell, or did she? As he watched, her expression changed again into one of resolve.

"Okay-James and I will give you one, and you can come over to the house and get Toby's, but call first."

Larkin agreed that he would do that and continued, "Did you notice anything suspicious from any of the help?"

"No, of course not," Cromwell said. "These people have worked for me for years. They are loyal. That is why I keep them."

"So, you haven't had words with any of them?"

"No."

"How did your wife get along with them?"

"They did what she asked."

"Let me put it the way: Did they like her?"

"How should I know what their feelings are? Hell, they may not like me."

Larkin decided to let that pass, but if he were a betting man, he would put his money on the not liking. He flashed a look at Cassie. She shrugged her shoulders.

"Mrs. White, the cook, does she live here at the house?"

"No, she and her husband live in town."

"Mrs. White at the lake with a gun." Cramer spoke so only Larkin could hear. He was remembering his game of Clue.

"What's the housekeeper's name?"

"Her name is Blanch Wilby."

"Do you have any servants that live here at the manor?"

"Only Harry Preston, my butler. His wife died years ago and he has stayed here at the house ever since. His wife, Mildred, used to be my housekeeper. Harry and I are pretty close."

Larkin wondered if they were close enough that Preston would cover up a murder for him, but kept his thoughts to himself.

"Are there any other full-time employees?"

"I have security people who control the gates. They work in the shack on the right side of the house. From that point, the monitoring system watches the entire house and grounds. It was the guard who opened the gates for you."

"Are there different guards or do you keep the same one all of the time?"

"I have two guards. One works the night shift, the other during the day. I insisted that the same people be sent every time."

"How long have they been here?"

"Since we got the new security system, in about 'ninety-eight, I'd say."

"I think we have about everything we need at this time," Larkin informed. "I will let you know when we have something. I don't suppose any of you are planning any long trips."

"Is this your way of telling us not to leave town, Detective?" Cromwell asked.

"I simply want to be aware if anyone has any plans to be out of town."

"I have a book signing in New York the fifteenth." It was Cassie Thompson. "I can always cancel if I need to."

"So, you're a writer, Ms. Thompson. Have you written anything I would be familiar with?"

The smile, which she seemed to always wear, broadened. "I write romantic novels, Mr. Larkin. I really doubt it."

"You do plan on coming back?" He ignored her last statement.

"I'll be back in three days, but under the circumstances, I can just cancel altogether."

Her dad assured her there was no need for that, but by her attitude, she had already decided not to go. None of the others had plans that would take them out of town, and after brief interviews with the servants Cramer and Larkin left the family alone.

On their way out, the two detectives stopped and interviewed the security guard, Jack Johnston, who had started his shift at 7 AM. He said that the guards made a log of everyone who came in or went out. On the Friday night in question, Mrs. Cromwell had left about nine o'clock - alone. He knew this because Max Daily, the other guard, had told him. He had also told Johnston that she was driving at a high rate of speed, as if she was upset. That wasn't his exact words, but Johnston had gotten the drift. He consulted his book and told Larkin it was 9:05 when she drove through the gates. When he asked if she had returned since, Johnston said she had not; at least, not while he was on duty.

When asked if he had noticed anyone out of the ordinary hanging around the premises he said no, but Larkin could tell that something was bothering him.

"If you think there is something the police ought to know, don't be afraid to say so."

"Well, I've been debating whether I should tell Mr. Cromwell about this for some time. The other guard told me the kids have been sneaking out the back. He has watched someone in a car, picking him or her up. I know they aren't supposed to be out late, but I don't think they know that anyone has seen them. Saturday night he saw the girl leave about ten and the boy left around eleven. They sneak along the brick wall to the big tree in the back. They have made footholds by breaking out some of the bricks. They're able to climb over the wall and down the tree. I checked it out to see how they were doing it," he said proudly.

This was interesting. Both Tina and Todd had said they were home all weekend. Larkin knew that kids did things like this: in fact, he himself had sneaked out after curfew. Was it just teen high jinks or something more sinister? Tomorrow he would check out their escape route and tell them he knew they lied. He made a mental note to interview the security guard who worked nights about the possibility of someone slipping onto the grounds to deliver the ransom note.

They were finally on their way home and Cramer knew he would soon have a shower, but he also knew he and Larkin were going to brainstorm all the way home. He knew this because he knew Larkin.

"Well. What do you think?" Larkin began.

"Her old man did it, pure and simple?"

"You think?"

"What husband has a wife missing since Friday evening and doesn't call the police until Tuesday morning? I know if my wife was missing, I'd be up to my neck in policemen."

"You heard Cromwell. The note said if the police were involved, they would kill her."

"How convenient," Cramer sniffed. "He didn't get the note until Sunday afternoon, yet he made no effort to find her." Ted threw a sideways glance at his boss. He never knew what Larkin was thinking, it was part of the game. His boss might be thinking the very same thing, but wouldn't let on. He wanted his men to think for themselves.

"What you're forgetting is that he has put up with her dramatics for twenty-odd years. Why kill her now?"

"How do you know she's dead?"

"Exactly," Larkin exclaimed. "This could be another one of her dramas."

"So, what you're saying is, Cromwell might not be too concerned because she has done this sort of thing before."

"Either is possible."

Cramer hated it when he did that. His boss would have him almost convinced of some scenario and then he would bring up another possibility.

"What you're not considering is, that he has put up with her shenanigans for all these years, and this time it was the last straw."

"Maybe," Larkin breathed, leaning his head back against the seat and closing his eyes. He would be able to think better if he was home.

"But you don't think so?"

"There is a lot of circumstantial evidence against Cromwell, but that gut feeling says he didn't do it. It's early yet; we'll see what tomorrow brings."

Cramer was quiet also, lost in his own thoughts. It was getting dark, and he had developed a headache. They had spent the entire day at the Cromwells', interviewing the family and servants. All he wanted to do was get home, grab a quick shower, and fall into bed. Larkin, on the other hand, was hours from going to bed. Cramer knew he would devour the notes he had taken and see if there were any discrepancies in the stories. He would go over the notes he had taken mentally, and add it to the observations he had made. Somehow, he could do the math and usually come up with a suspect.

"I still think our best suspect is the old man," Cramer said into the silence.

"What about the kids?"

"The kids loved their mother. Besides, what would be their motive?"

"Off hand, I can see about a million reasons for committing murder."

That was definitely true. Cramer had been a police officer long enough to know money did crazy things to people.

"The kids just seemed to be very upset."

"So did Cromwell."

"All I'm saying is his actions don't back up what he says he's feeling."

"I believe there are at least two people involved," Larkin said.

"What about Cromwell and his older daughter?"

That struck a raw nerve. Larkin didn't like the idea of Cassie Thompson being involved at all.

"I mean, they do seem awfully close, and I get the feeling that the woman isn't fond of her step-mother."

Larkin had the same feeling, but that didn't mean she was involved in this.

"I believe that there were two people involved. They wanted the money divided so they could make a quick getaway."

"It may be one person, with the two bags just to throw us off."

"Anything is possible," Larkin agreed.

"Hell, I don't know. Maybe the kidnapper just wanted to walk balanced when he left the boat."

Larkin smiled. He could always tell when Cramer was tiring of the game, but he was always good for a laugh. Larkin kept him around for entertainment.

"If he wanted rid of her, why not divorce?"

"From hearing her family talk, I don't think the lady would have gone quietly. A million dollars might have been cheap to get rid of her."

"Maybe. What we need to do is find the body."

"If she's dead."

"If she's dead," Larkin agreed. "You're learning to listen to people not just hear. We know her family believes she might have set this up herself."

"Why not?" Cramer shrugged his shoulders. "She and the old man have a fight; she wants to make him suffer... "

They were nearing Larkin's house, and he held up a hand to stop Cramer. "I plan on doing more interviews with the family again tomorrow. I want you to check on their banking activity. Let's check on all of the servants too. Look for any large deposits in their checking or savings. See if anyone purchased bonds or CDs."

"Good idea. We're looking for the money trail, right?"

"The money is the key. We find it, we find the kidnapper."

"The guys at the lake are going to be shutting down pretty soon. They will start looking for Mrs. Cromwell again at daybreak."

"I was hoping they would find her body if she was there..."

"It was storming Monday night. She might have washed downstream... "

Larkin had gotten out of the car. "I'll see you tomorrow," he said, before Cramer pulled away.

CHAPTER 3

———— ◆ ————

Larkin sat at his desk, a big cup of coffee in front of him, realizing he was getting old. His head felt like he was suffering from a hangover. He hadn't felt this bad since he was young and boozing the night away. He had only slept about three hours and it had caught up with him this morning. He had kept going over and over the family's interviews and just couldn't come up with anything. This wasn't like him.

Because Ted had lost sleep, he was as grumpy as Larkin's ex-wife. Today he passed on the rolls, saying his stomach was queasy, and fixed himself a cup of black coffee instead.

He seated himself in the chair next to Larkin's desk "Tell me you know who the kidnapper is so we can take the day off and get some rest."

"I'm good, but not that good." Larkin sat back in his chair and let the hot liquid slide down his throat, hoping it would bring him back to life.

"Are our plans still the same?"

"Unless something happens to change them. The guys are back working the lake. I got a call from the chief of police, just before you came in."

Cramer shook his head and took a sip of his own coffee. "Kim and I had a fight last night."

That was another reason for the blue mood, Larkin figured. "Was it because you were late?"

"I'm always late, boss. Ever since I started working for you."

"Do you want to transfer out?" Larkin smiled for he knew the answer before he asked.

"Hell no. You're the best and everyone knows it. I've learned more in the last two years, working with you, than in my entire career... Besides, I worked my tail off to get here."

Larkin never had a chance to learn what the fight was about, for just then David Blake, head of forensics, showed up in his office carrying some papers.

"It's not seven yet," Ted moaned. "Why can't you be like all the other science guys, and take weeks to do your job?"

"The others don't have Larkin breathing down their necks."

"What do you have?" Larkin held out his hand for the papers.

He quickly scanned the results of the DNA testing on the Cromwell family and the employees. "Are you sure!" he exclaimed.

"Have you ever known me to be wrong?"

Larkin hadn't. The man was as good at his job as people claimed.

Most of the blood in the car belonged to Mrs. Cromwell, but a smudge left on the steering column matched the DNA on the ransom envelope. The blood didn't match any of the family or employees. David said it would take a few days to run it through CODIS, a program to exchange and compare DNA profiles on a national level.

David believed Julie had fought with her attacker. He also felt there wasn't enough blood loss in her car to cause her death. There had been no fingerprints found in the car, not even hers. The evidence said the assault had started in her car, and she had probably jumped out and ran. He believed after Julie vacated the car her assailant took time to wipe down the inside, but in the dark, he had missed the spot of blood.

"Could he have been wearing gloves?" Ted asked.

"He could have been. Maybe his prints are on file and he knows he will be easily identified," Larkin said.

Larkin and Cramer were shocked to learn that neither of the younger children belonged to Cromwell; but the greatest shock of all was, the same man fathered Julie and her son.

"Are we talking about incest here?" Larkin exclaimed.

"That's what I would call it. She and her son both belong to her father."

"Whew!" Larkin let out his breath.

"The girl doesn't belong to Lawrence Cromwell either."

"Does the girl also belong to Julie's father?" Cramer asked.

"The girl belongs to neither man."

"Another curious point is there were two sets of prints lifted from the ransom note. One set belonged to Cromwell and the other to his daughter, Tina.

"The saliva taken from the flap doesn't belong to any family member, or any of the Cromwell's employees."

After Blake left the office it was Ted that spoke first. "I wonder if Cromwell knew there had been a strange rooster in the hen house."

"A strange rooster in the hen house'?" Larkin repeated.

"It's just something my grandpa always said."

"It will be interesting to see his reaction when I bring it up," Larkin said.

"We're going to be awakening a lot of sleeping dogs on this one," Cramer quipped.

"It does seem like the more we find out the more confusing it gets," Larkin admitted.

Cramer took out his notes and scanned though then. "Cromwell said he was the only one to touch the note, as far as he knew. So, how did Tina's fingerprints get on the envelope? That's a good question and I plan on asking it tomorrow."

"Maybe she saw it first and picked it up out of curiosity."

"If that is the case, seeing that it was addressed to her dad, why wouldn't she give it to him instead of putting it back on the floor?"

"I think that she would," Cramer nodded.

"So do I," Larkin said. "She lied about going out Saturday night also. Remember what the guard said."

"So did her brother. The security guy said they both snuck out of the house."

"Kids do things like that, and they lie to keep from getting caught. Is it just kids being kids, or something more? Then there is the DNA they took from the flap. It doesn't belong to any member of the family."

"We know we have at least one outsider involved Ted said. "But how are we going to find out whom?"

Larkin sighed. "I have a feeling we're in for a long one this time."

"Well, if Mrs. Cromwell herself was involved, she sure went to a lot of trouble," Cramer said.

"One thing for sure. If she planned it something went wrong."

"She could have refused to give her accomplice the money."

Larkin slapped him on the shoulder. "Now you' re thinking like a detective."

Just then, the phone rang. Cramer picked it up. "It's the guys at the lake," he put his hand over the receiver to talk to Larkin. "They think they've found her." He hung up after assuring them that they would be right there.

The day was dark and overcast - and an undesirable odor assaulted Larkin's nostrils as he stepped out of the car. He had always hated the smell of fish and polluted water. His dad had insisted on teaching him to fish when he as a kid; something else he disliked. It brought back unpleasant memories. Now, if he added the smell of a dead body, he had the murder scene. Some veteran police offers got used to the smell, Larkin never had.

Up ahead they could see two rival TV news crews, straining to see beyond the yellow tape.

"Oh no," Larkin said. "The sharks are circling."

"I'm shocked that it's taken this long," Cramer said.

"Oh great," Larkin said as they walked closer.

"Your favorite reporter, I believe." Cramer smiled.

Molly Jenkins could track a story like a bloodhound and had the attitude of a pit bull with PMS.

"I was hoping she wouldn't get wind of this for a while," Larkin said through clinched teeth.

"Come on, old buddy," Cramer said, slapping him on the back. "You know it had to happen sooner or later."

As Larkin lifted the tape that roped off the crime scene, Molly caught his arm. "Is it true they've found the body of Julie Cromwell, Detective?"

Larkin stopped dead still. He hated reporters in general and Molly in particular. "Give me a break, Jenkins. I haven't even gotten to the scene yet." He shook loose from her grip. He would like to make her eat her microphone, but there were cameras rolling and she wasn't worth losing his job.

"If you're still here after I finish my investigation, I'll give you a statement."

"Oh, I'll be here, Detective," she called after him, "and if I don't get one, I'll have to make one up."

"Easy, man," Cramer caught hold of him. "Don't let her get in under your skin. Let's go do our jobs."

David Blake and his crew pulled in and parked beside Larkin's car, and the two detectives waited for them to battle their way through the reporters. They all walked together to where the body was lying on the deck covered with a tarp.

There were people gawking and trying to strain by the officers securing the scene. Yellow tape kept the crowd from coming near the deck. The two local news crews tried to be the first to get the story.

Larkin and Ted watched as the head of forensics made his preliminary examination. Larkin could see a bruise on her left cheek and a gash in her head, possibly the reason for the blood in her car. She also had a bullet hole between her eyes.

Larkin visually took a picture of the scene before stepping aside to hear what the officer in charge of the diving operation had to say.

"The body is pretty well preserved, as you can see. It's probably because of the cold water. We found her almost under the dock; her clothing caught on a hook in one of the deck posts. We would have found her sooner, but we figured the storm moved her further than it did. We also found what we think is the murder weapon. It looks like the killer stood on the dock and flung it into the lake as far as he could." He called to one of his men to bring the revolver in question, which was already in a plastic bag and labeled, handing it to Larkin.

Larkin looked at it for a second. "Looks like a .38 Smith and Wesson service revolver."

"It is. There's a full load with two spent brass in the cylinder. Someone shot her twice: Once in the head, once through the heart. Whoever killed her knew what they were doing."

"We'll know more about the gun after Barry Talbot examines it." The officer shook his head. Talbot knew his firearms. The man first became interested while he was in the service and had studied guns for thirty years.

"Were there fingerprints on the weapon?"

"We didn't test it yet, but my guess is you won't find any. If there had been, the water would have washed them away."

"Give it to David and have him dust it while they're checking the boat," Larkin said.

The *Sea Angel* rocked gently in the breeze, while Blake and his men scoured it for usable prints. The perpetrator left no evidence on the tarp, or surrounding area.

David Blake carefully removed the revolver and dusted it for prints, but gave up after a while and looked toward Larkin shaking his head.

About the best they could hope for now was that Talbot could tell them if it was the murder weapon.

"The gun doesn't look like it's been in the water long," the officer concluded.

"What do you think?" Larkin asked as David looked up from where he was leaning over the corpse.

"I think she was a victim of a sexual assault. Her sweater is torn at the neckline She took a beating, but that isn't what killed her. I think a man's fist caused the bruise on her cheek, and his ring was responsible for the cut on the side of her forehead. It is only a superficial wound, but head wounds cause a lot of blood. She has a bullet in her chest, and one in her head - either would have proved fatal. The killer shot her in the chest at close range, and when she fell, he stepped closer and put a bullet through her brain. Her nails are broken and it looks like there may be skin under them. I'll know more after the autopsy. I hope her being in the lake didn't destroy the evidence," David said.

"Can you tell where the murder occurred?"

"It looks like where we're standing. I sprayed the dock with luminol and it glowed pretty well. We have blood smeared from where we're standing to the end of the deck. I think she was facing her killer when it happened.

"After he shot her, he threw the gun in the lake, and rolled his victim in right behind it. I don't believe the killer is very strong. If he had been, he would have carried her to the end of the dock."

"So, you're saying he struggled with the body. Could the murderer have been a woman?"

"He could have been, or a small man," David said. "A body is dead weight; even though the victim is small, dead weight is hard to deal with."

The storm Tuesday night had destroyed most of the evidence. They would have to take the body back to the station and air dry her clothes, as well as other evidence found there. Larkin hoped David could give them something to work with.

Larkin and Cramer stopped on the way back to the car and faced the press. Larkin kept it simple, and appealed to them to keep it off the news until they could notify the family.

"We have recovered the body of Julie Cromwell."

"How did she die?" Molly asked.

"She was shot."

"So she was murdered?"

"We are treating it as a homicide."

"Do you have any suspects?"

"Not at this time," Larkin said, walking away.

"What else do you know?" Molly followed him.

"That is all I can tell you." Larkin and Cramer pushed their way through the screaming reporters to get to their car.

The CSU team photographed the body before removing it and taking it back to the lab beside the police station. The new building, which also housed the Springfield Police Department, had a new science lab that was heaven to a man like David Blake, who had made forensics his life.

David stopped at Larkin's car to talk a minute, before they moved her. "We didn't find much, I'm afraid. The cause of death is obvious.

Someone shot her once in the heart and once in the head. Either wound would have proved fatal."

"Do you have a time of death?"

"Couldn't tell by liver temperature, but I'd venture to say she's been dead between twenty-four to forty-eight hours. I'll know more after we autopsy her."

"If it was over a dispute about the ransom, as we believe, it probably happened Tuesday morning about three o'clock right after Cromwell delivered the money.

"It fits," Blake confirmed.

Larkin was confident in their CSU team. For a town no bigger than Springfield they had a good one. It had come together by accident and a combination of David Blake campaigning until he had people he could work well with. David knew that it meant the difference in having a good police force and having a great one.

Barry Talbot was their firearms expert, who was self-taught. David Blake came to them from a crime lab in California. His parents were from the Springfield area, and when they had become ill, David moved his family back home, bringing his expertise with him. To Larkin, David was the best, and he should know. Before, he had to travel to bigger cities with bigger labs and wait what seemed like forever for them to analyze evidence for him. Now, he only had to go next door. David Blake had fought hard to get the city to build the crime lab they had now. He even organized fund raisers and solicited donations from the public. He had given talks in little neighboring towns telling them that there would be help for them in solving their toughest crimes He had kept that promise, and therefore was so busy that it sometimes took longer for him to get to their own crimes. Larkin didn't complain though, because he remembered how it was before David came.

He organized his little band of experts-some educated, some self-taught- but all knew what they were doing. His little gang would swoop in on a crime scene, each knowing their job. They would collect the evidence, take photographs, tag and bag and take notes on every piece of evidence. David even kept a diary anticipating questions a shrewd defense attorney might ask.

Harry Merts, their medical examiner, also proved an asset. David had stolen him from another police department after talking his superiors into replacing the man they had.

Henry Clay, the man they had when he first came, wasn't well trained and resented David, who was. He didn't have a good working relationship with the police department. David constantly asked the police chief to find someone comfortable working with the investigators. He said a good medical examiner could guide the detectives in the right direction, but Henry Clay only showed them the door. The man even growled if Larkin or one of his men stood in on an autopsy.

One day, Larkin put a bug in the district attorney's ear. He told Deets, if they had the right team, they would be able to solve more crimes and Deets would *have* a better chance of being governor. With any luck, they could kill two birds with one stone. They could get the man David wanted for the job, and ship Deets out of their jurisdiction. Soon afterward, David had his man.

Merts was recovering from a nasty divorce, so he couldn't wait to get away-and the rest, as they say, is history.

Harry was probably the funniest person in the department and didn't care if the sun shined tomorrow. He got his kicks out of watching macho police officers who had never seen an autopsy performed. They would either find themselves on the floor, or leave with their hand over their mouth heaving. It was not because of the sight, as much as the smell involved.

Larkin always opted for a gas mask, even though Harry told him if he would tolerate the smell for about three minutes, the olfactory nerves would go numb and he could no longer smell. The trouble with that was, he couldn't stand it that long.

Sawing a skull or splitting a corpse stem to stern never seemed to bother old Harry, no matter what condition the body. His post mortem humor was a legend around the station. Larkin knew it would offend most civilians, but for the people who worked homicide it was a defense mechanism. It kept the people who worked with murder every day from going insane.

Larkin would have to inform Cromwell that his wife had been found and ask him to identify the body. It was only a formality, however, because he recognized her from pictures that he saw at the house yesterday. The divers had also found a purse with her identification as well as the gun.

"Do you want me to go to the Cromwells' with you?" Cramer asked.

"No. I'd rather you get to work tracing the money. I'll go out to Cromwell's. I want to see his reaction when I tell him."

"I got you," Cramer said. There was always a method to Larkin's madness.

CHAPTER 4

Cromwell opened the door, looking as though he hadn't sleep in days. When Larkin told him the bad news the blood drained from his face, leaving him an ashy pale. He sagged into a chair, deep gut-wrenching sobs shaking his body. Larkin was tempted to put his arm around him to comfort him. Either he was devastated, or he was the best actor Larkin had ever seen. After witnessing his reaction, Larkin was glad he didn't give him the news by phone.

"I will need you to come down to the morgue to identify her."

"Of course." Cromwell tried to pull himself together. He took a handkerchief out of his pocket and mopped his nose and eyes.

"Maybe you would like Mrs. Thompson to do it for you," Larkin suggested.

"No-no... I want to see her," his voice caught.

"What's the matter, Daddy?" Tina asked as she and Todd came into the room.

Cromwell rose and embrace them both.

"It's Mom, isn't it?" Tina began to cry. "They've found her, haven't they?"

"Yes, honey, they have. I'm sorry."

The family huddled together while Larkin put through a call to Cassie Thompson. After asking how her dad was doing, she assured him she would be there as soon as possible.

While they awaited her arrival, Larkin reflected. He needed to ask many questions, but this was neither the time nor the place. He would give the family a few days to compose themselves then he would be back.

Larkin had been there when Cromwell and his daughter had viewed the body. It took a toll on Cassie as she watched her father go through such misery, and Larkin wished he had been able to shield her from such pain. He wouldn't even let himself wonder why.

Larkin and Cramer attended the funeral to see if anyone suspicious showed up.

The people in attendance were mostly family. A few of Mr. Cromwell's co-workers came by to pay their respects.

Cromwell was in his own world, not really comprehending what was going on around him. Cassie sat with her arms around Tina and Todd. The children were taking it hard, like any child who had lost their mother.

The Risners and their son, Toby attended. When Larkin saw the boy, a feeling washed over him he couldn't define. It was like something he knew, but just couldn't quite grasp. Before he could recapture it, someone had come up to him, causing it to evaporate into thin air. It frustrated him, but the reality refused to resurrect.

Larkin and Cramer spent the next few days behind the scenes. The gun found at the murder site proved to be the murder weapon. There were no prints on it, however; either proving they washed away or the person who pulled the trigger had worn gloves.

David Blake again went over how the evidence related to the crime. The attack started in the car. Her attacker ripper her sweater at the neckline, and hit her in the face with his fist, causing bruising to her left cheek. David Blake also believed the gash in her head had been made by the man's ring, causing the blood evidence in the car. She had hair and skin under the broken nails, proving she had put up a fight. David Blake believed she had jumped from the car after fighting with her assailant, but like himself, David wasn't convinced that her attacker had been the one who fired the fatal shot. What neither of them could understand was why she had run toward the dock instead of the woods surrounding the lake, when it would have offered her more cover. It must have been that she panicked. Larkin thought there was another person involved, and Julie must have run toward him. Maybe she recognized the person and she believed he would help her. Instead, he shot her through the heart. Cramer was still convinced it was her husband, and Larkin had to admit she would have trusted him above all others.

Two pieces of the puzzle came together after Blake was finished. The DNA from Julie's broken nails and the saliva from the flap of the envelope belonged to the same person. Now all they had to do was find the person.

It had been a week since Karl had any contact with the Cromwell family. He had called this morning and set up a time to meet with them, around one o'clock; but before that, he wanted to speak with the security guard that worked nights. He wanted to know if the man would be willing to give them a DNA sample. Someone knew the place well enough to be able to deliver a letter to the front door in broad daylight. The guard would be perfect person. He was supposed to be watching the place and no one would pay attention to him. They might just get lucky and find the mysterious donor of the envelope.

Cramer phoned him on the way to work and told him two different family members had deposited a large amount of money. This was just days after the kidnapping. The bank wouldn't give any other information without a court order. Larkin told him to hold off on getting the order until he had a chance to interview the people involved. He wanted to see their reaction when he mentioned the money. It shocked Larkin to find out who they were. One was James Risner, and the other was Cassie Thompson.

When Larkin asked Cromwell if the family would be available for an interview, he had said yes, and asked if he should have Cassie there as well. Karl told him no. He wanted to question the older daughter alone. He wanted to talk about some things he knew she would be more open about if the others weren't present. The money was one of them.

Ted came in at starting time and they began going over the developments in the case as well as their plans for the day.

"James Risner deposited exactly half a million into his account the day after Julie Cromwell's funeral." Ted winked.

"Interesting," Karl agreed. Ted had received his full attention. "What about Cassie?" That was the one that concerned him the most.

"Your girlfriend only put in a quarter of a mil," Ted said.

"Humph," Larkin grunted. "My girlfriend." He wasn't sure what floored him the most. The fact that Cassie Thompson had that much money, or that Ted had picked up on the attraction he felt for her.

"You have the hots for her," Ted laughed. "Admit it."

"She's attractive." Karl was still not willing to commit himself.

"She's damn hot and you know it." Ted seemed to find it amusing.

"And by what we just found out she might be an accomplice to murder."

"Walk easy, boss. I've never seen you react to a woman you're investigating. I really don't want to see you get hurt."

"Thanks, Cramer, but you know me. I always remain objective."

He tried to sound confident, but found it difficult to believe himself. A feeling in the pit of his stomach said he cared way too much, whether she was involved or not.

"I have a scenario, if you would like to hear it."

"Shoot."

"What if Cassie Thompson was fed up with the way her stepmother was treating her dad? She hires James Risner to help her get rid of Julie. Since they're afraid that suspicion will fall on them, they hire an actual hit man, the one with the foreign DNA, to do the killing. He does the woman in, Cassie Thompson pays him a quarter of a million out of her share, and they all go happily about their own business."

"After we interview them we will know if we need to subpoena their bank records," Larkin said. He was reluctant to force the issue unless they refused.

"There was also a check written on Risner's account for $100,000."

"It could have been the killer wanted more money."

"You mean the killer might be blackmailing them."

"If it happened like you think. Sure he could be. He might be thinking he has a money tree for life. Another option is that he wanted 350,000 to do the job, and Ms. Thompson made Risner come up with the rest. Another version could be that Risner hired the man himself and Cassie had nothing to do with it."

"What does she do for a living?" Ted asked.

"She is a creator of romantic fiction. In other words she writes love stories."

Somehow, he knew Larkin would remember. "Do you honestly believe that mushy dribble makes her the big bucks?" Ted questioned.

Karl didn't, but he refused to say so. "What about a contractor? in this town, do you think he makes six figures on his deals?"

Ted frowned as he stared at his boss. The man had it bad. His attitude turned defensive every time he mentioned the woman in a negative light.

"I can't imagine either of them making that kind of money," Ted agreed. There would have to be more investigating before they could get a clear picture of what was going on.

"I plan to interview Cassie Thompson this evening. I will ask her about the money and see what she has to say."

"Want me to come along?" Ted asked.

"No." He spoke quickly, causing Ted to wonder if he wanted to be alone with the woman. "I plan on interviewing the younger children about their sneaking out Saturday night, and about how Tina's fingerprints got on the envelope. After that I plan on going to Cassie Thompson's and interviewing her. I want you to go over to Cromwell's medical practice and interview the people who work for him. See if anyone accuses him of having an affair. We just aren't seeing some avenue yet. We will go together to interview the Risners tomorrow."

"You figure it might turn into a hostile environment?"

"It could be. She certainly didn't want us to test her son's DNA."

"Maybe infidelity runs in the family," Ted said.

"All I know is, I want someone along for a witness when I interview her. When I talked to her the other night, she looked at me like she would like to bite my head off."

"Scared?" Cramer laughed.

"Uneasy—I'd like to think."

"It's time," Ted consulting his watch, rising to leave.

"I'll see you back here around five. If I haven't made it back yet, go on home and I will see you tomorrow."

CHAPTER 5

---◆---

L arkin arrive at twelve-thirty at the Cromwell place. Max Daily buzzed him in. The guard usually worked nights, but had traded shifts with Jack Johnston for the day. He looked surprised to see Larkin get out of his car and head toward the shack.

He was a gorilla, was the first thought to hit the detective. This guy could put the hurt on somebody. Karl wondered if it might be his DNA they were looking for.

The two men introduced themselves, and Daily offered Karl a seat, turning on his swiveling stool away from the cameras to face Larkin.

"I was wondering how hard it is to keep an eye on the entire property from here."

Daily showed him the different screens and angles the camera picked up and told him, 'I see what is going on in every spot inside of these gates."

Larkin sat on the stool beside him. "From what I see, it would be close to impossible to get to the front door in daylight, and put a letter through the mail slot." He swiveled to face Max.

"I'll go a step farther. I'd say it was impossible. There is no way on Johnson's watch, or mine either."

"You know that Mr. Cromwell found a note that looked to have been put through the mail slot?"

"Yes—I've heard that."

"But you don't believe it."

"If someone delivered a letter that day, it was someone inside the house."

"It could be anyone in the family then," Larkin said, "or anyone who worked for them. It could even be you, Mr. Daily."

Larkin waited for the man to beat him to a bloody pulp, and was relieved to hear him laugh instead. "It could have been. I had the opportunity; but it wasn't me, Mr. Larkin."

"Would you mind giving us a sample of your DNA?"

"You don't have to take blood, do you? There ain't anybody coming at me with a needle."

Larkin had to smile when he thought of a man as big as this one being afraid to be stuck.

"No. Actually, all I have to do is swab the inside of your mouth." He produced the plastic bag from the inside of his pocket.

"Sounds painless." He stood still while Larkin took the sample, all the time scanning the screens to see if all points were covered.

Larkin had to agree with Daily. The guards would have seen anyone who came at the door.

"Did you by any chance let anyone other than the immediate family through that gate the day in question?" The thought had just occurred to him.

"As a matter of fact, I let the Risner boy—what's his name."

"Toby," Larkin supplied.

"Yeah—I don't know why I can't ever remember that kid's name."

"So you let him in that day?"

"Yes—it was another day I traded with Johnston."

"Are you sure it was him?"

"Yeah, he drove in about eleven o'clock. He didn't stay but about fifteen minutes and I let him out. He had a different car, and I didn't recognize him at first. It was some kind of a sports car. All I know is, it looked new and expensive. He pulled right up to the door and I walked out to meet him."

"And it was him?"

"It was him all right. I know him when I see him. I just can't remember his name."

Larkin had definitely decided to interview Toby and get a sample of his DNA. Red flags were going up all around him. He wondered what a boy in college was doing buying a brand-new car. He could have asked Tina to make sure she put the note where her dad could find it, and that's why her fingerprints were found on it. There was something about that boy that Larkin couldn't put his finger on. He had only been around him briefly at the funeral, but ever since he'd had a nagging feeling that things were not the way they seemed.

The case was progressing slowly, but it was still moving forward. Larkin tried not to get frustrated. What was it Ted had said? The more they found out, the less they knew, or something to that effect. Larkin was tempted to agree with him, but he had seen cases before that seemed to be going nowhere and then one lead would bring it all together.

After seeing how tight security was, Larkin was convinced a family member had brought the letter in. it had to be Mrs. Cromwell herself, or someone who worked at the estate. It had to be an insider; someone Cromwell trusted, or Cromwell himself.

At one o'clock Larkin was in the Cromwell living room. "Thanks for seeing me again," Larkin shook hands with Cromwell. "There are just a few loose ends I need to tie up before you call the children."

"It sounds serious."

"It is."

"All right." Cromwell seemed a little uneasy, but he took a seat and offered Larkin one.

"There is no easy way for me to ask this; Mr. Cromwell..."

"Please, call me Larry, if you don't mind. My father was Mr. Cromwell, and he's dead."

"Only if you call me Karl." Larkin reached forward and they shook on it. "You may change your mind when you find out what I have to tell you."

"I think I can handle whatever it is after what happened to Julie..."

"When we did the DNA test on the children..." Larkin paused.

"You found out that Todd wasn't mine, right?"

"I know this has to be hard for you," Larkin breathed.

"Julie became pregnant while we were going together. We had never had sex and when I confronted her about it, she told me she'd been raped."

"So you knew."

"Yes, I did," he said hanging his head.

"Did you know that Tina is not your child either?" It was hard posing that question to a man Larkin was beginning to like.

"I didn't know for sure…" He raised his head and Larkin could see the pain in his eyes.

"May I ask you a personal question? Why would you stay with her knowing this?"

"I don't expect you to understand," Larry breathed. "You don't know the demons that chased her."

Larkin was sorry to dreg up such pain, when some of it was starting to go away.

"My wife and her sister were abused as children. It did something to both of them."

"Who abused them?"

"It was their father—the bastard. I hope he rots in hell."

"I suppose you knew then who Todd's father was?"

"Yes, I did."

Larkin had never seen the man react so vehemently. "Did they report him?"

"They were just children and they lived in a small backwoods town where people tend to look the other way. I wanted to take him to court, but Julie and Carrie both said no. They just wanted to forget it ever happened. The trouble was, she couldn't forget."

"The abuse was obviously sexual; were they physically abused as well?"

"I have said all I'm going to say about that, Karl. My wife never wanted it known, and out of respect to her, I won't discuss it."

"I can understand that, but do you think that it could be someone from her past who is involved in this?"

"I really don't think so." His brow furrowed as he thought about it "When the girls left, they never let anyone know where they were, and as far as I know, no one ever tried to find them."

"Maybe their father found out you had money and decided on a way to get it."

"I really don't think so, but I suppose it could be possible."

Larkin didn't believe so either. It wasn't her father's DNA under her nails: Blake would have found it. The way Cromwell talked, the man never traveled from the area, but he could have involved someone else in the scheme with the promise of half a million dollars. It was something he would look into. He had never worked a case where there were so many possibilities. He had never found himself clutching at straws, as he was doing now.

"My wife was very insecure. She felt that no one loved her, that she was unlovable. I couldn't prove I loved her no matter how hard I tried." His voice caught.

Larkin patted his shoulder. "It wasn't your fault. I'd say you did all you could."

"I did all that I knew to do, but unfortunately it wasn't enough."

"Could we get the children now?" Larkin broke in. "I still need to interview your oldest daughter and get to the office."

Cromwell asked his butler to call the children. If he was curious about what Larkin wanted, he didn't ask.

"You won't tell them about what you found out, will you?" His eyes pleaded with the detective.

"I see no need for doing that," Karl assured him.

Larry seemed relieved, but Karl wondered if he would remain that way after he heard the line of questioning he intended.

Tina and Todd shuffled in looking half-asleep. He didn't think either was used to getting out of bed before evening. Larkin guessed it was easy to sleep when you were out all night. He had examined the place where they had cut out foot holes in the wall. On the other side next to the fence, there was a big tree next to the wall. The limbs formed a natural stairway to the top of the wall. The letter carrier could have gotten in that way, but how could he have made it to the front door without someone seeing him? It had to be an inside job.

"Hi," Larkin greeted the unhappy faces as they took seats on the couch close to where their dad sat. Cromwell looked better today and so did the children. At least they seemed to be coping.

Tina grunted, but Todd didn't bother to speak.

"I know you both want to catch whoever did this to your mother," Larkin began.

They both nodded their heads.

"There are few things I need to understand before I can do that. I'll start with you, Tina. You know that we dusted the envelope for fingerprints?"

She shook her head and he continued. "We found your dad's and we also found yours."

Tina gasped. Todd's eyes flew directly to hers.

"See here, Larkin," Cromwell started to rise from his chair, but Larkin motioned for him to sit back down.

"Your dad said he never showed the note to anyone but the police. Can you explain how your fingerprints got there?"

Every eye turned toward her, causing her to squirm nervously in her seat.

"Okay—okay," she said at last. "I was the one who put the note there."

"Where did it come from?" her father blurted out. "Did you have anything to do with putting this thing together?"

Larkin put up his hand again to stop Larry.

"My mom gave me the note and told me she was going to teach my father a lesson. She said if I helped her, she would buy me that dress I wanted for the prom. I'm only a sophomore and a senior invited me to go. The dress I wanted cost three hundred dollars and at first she said no..." She was babbling so that it was becoming hard to understand.

"Tina, we need you to focus." Larkin's voice was stern. "Just tell us in your own words what happened."

"My mom said for me to wait until Sunday and put the note where it looked like it came through the mail slot. She said if I did that, she would get me the dress. I have a date with the star quarterback," she whimpered.

"Did she tell you what was in the note?" Larkin tried to keep her on track.

"No, she didn't." Tina was in tears by now. "All I wanted was the dress, so I said I would do it. I didn't know she was going to be murdered."

"It's all right, honey." Cromwell had risen from his chair and gone to put his arm around her. "It's not your fault."

"Did she say anyone else was helping with the plan?"

"No—no, she just asked me to do it, and I did. She told me she was going away for a little while, and when she came back things would be different. She kissed me good-bye and she left."

If Tina was telling the truth, Julie Cromwell had planned the whole thing. Her family believed it was possible. Somehow, things went wrong and she didn't come back.

"Tina's really upset, Larkin. Can't we finish this another time?" her dad asked.

"I only have a few more questions, and we need to get this all out in the open. I want this case solved as badly as you do," Larkin informed him. "Besides, there are some things you need to know about both children."

Cromwell wilted. It was if he knew it was more bad news and he didn't know if he could take it.

"I talked to both of your security guards, and the night watchman saw Tina sneak out of the house Saturday around midnight and get into a car."

"You did what?" Cromwell's voice rose.

"I'm afraid I'm going to have to ask her where she went and who she was with," Larkin said.

"Tell him, Tina," Cromwell ordered.

"I was with my boyfriend, Snake."

"I told you that bum was a loser," Todd yelled at her.

"What about you," Tina yelled back. "You went out too."

"That's right, Todd," Larkin said. "The night guard busted you both."

"I wonder why he didn't tell me," Larry fumed.

"I'm afraid before he could, I told him to hold off until I had a chance to talk to the family." It was only a small lie, and with the mood Cromwell was in, he might fire the man. Larkin felt no need to tell their dad they had been guilty several times. By the look on Cromwell's face, Larkin doubted it would ever happen again.

"At least I'm of age." Todd said.

"You're still under my roof, and you will follow my rules as long as that is the case," his father told him. The boy's jaw clinched, but he said nothing.

"Let's get back to you, Tina. Where did you and your boyfriend go?"

"We went to the Paris Club."

Larkin knew the place was a popular hangout for teens. The young people could buy mixed drinks that were non-alcoholic, and dance to a live band. He himself would never have approved of a place like that. To Larkin is just paved the way for young people to become familiar with the bar scene. Modern parents were much different than his had been. They seemed cool with it. From the look on Larry's face, Larkin was convinced he had the same upbringing as his own.

"I don't want you hanging around a place like that," Cromwell raked his finger through his hair.

"I was only there about five minutes, Daddy."

"Why did you leave?" Larkin asked.

"Snake and I saw Todd and his friend come in. I knew he would throw a fit if he saw us so we sneaked out."

"Did you see your sister?" Larkin shot a direct look at Todd.

"No—I didn't."

"Where did you and Snake go from there?" The guard said you didn't get home until after three o'clock.

Tina hung her head. "Bobby's parents weren't home so we went back to his place. We played some video games and made out a little, and then he took me home."

On seeing her dad's face, she told him, "We didn't have sex, Daddy. I swear."

Larkin figured it was time to take the heat off Tina.

"What about you and your friend, Todd? What did you do?"

"We danced with a few girls, listened to the music awhile and then we went our separate ways. I came home, and I assume Kyle did the same."

"I will need the name and addresses of both of your friends," Larkin said.

"What are you going to do?" Todd worried. "Kyle's dad will skin him alive."

"This is an ongoing investigation, son. We will be checking out any lead. By the way, do either of your buddies have a police record?"

"Kyle doesn't," Todd put in rapidly. "I can't speak for that skuzz ball Tina hangs out with."

"He has a few minor offences," Tina admitted. "One time he was picked up for shoplifting."

"That's not so minor," Larkin informed her.

"He was hungry. He stole some snack cakes. His parents are never home and there is never any food in his house," she explained.

"Well, I guess I have everything I need from you two if you want to go."

They both wanted to go and they did.

"Thanks," Larry said after they had gone.

"For what?"

"For not saying anything about..."

Larkin waved it away. "It should come from you, if they're told."

"I haven't been to work since this happened." He walked over to the window and looked out. "All the matters to me now are my children."

"Well you sell your practice?" Larkin had gone to stand with him.

"No, I'll hire a couple of good surgeons to take my place. I have some prospects in mind. One works for the burn center in Columbus. He donates a lots of his time to people who can't afford to pay. I think that is something I would like to look into for our company. I could offer him a more lucrative salary and still allow him to do the same work."

"That's wonderful," Larkin exclaimed. It made him happy to see that some good might come from this mess.

"I hope you don't judge Julie to harshly." Larry had walked Karl, who was getting ready to leave, to the door.

"I try to reserve judgement of people. We're all made up of the things good and bad that have touched our lives."

"I tried to get her help," Larry said. "She went through psychiatrist after psychiatrist; it was just too painful for her to relive those memories of the past."

Larkin put his hand on Larry's shoulder, and looked deeply into his eyes. "You need to give yourself a break. You did all that you could."

"I should have found a way," he said at last.

"You know guilt is such a wasted emotion," Larkin told him.

"I'm going to retire," Larry said at last. "I'm going to devote my time to Tina and Todd. They need me now a lot more than my patients do."

"I agree. I hope things work out for all of you."

CHAPTER 6

———◦◆◦———

Driving toward Cassie Thompson's, Larkin thought about what he had said to Cromwell. He had meant it. If ever a family deserved a new beginning, this one did.

He had learned a major piece of the puzzle today. Julie Cromwell had set up her own kidnapping. Tina had delivered the note, not realizing she was helping set her mother up for murder. When he got back from Cassie Thompson's he would have David Blake run the mysterious stranger's DNA through the database again to see if there were any matches. One day he would get lucky and he would find one. All it took was a little patience.

Larkin couldn't wait to start brainstorming with Ted after what he had just learned. They usually went over everything in the morning before work, but if he finished early at Cassie's he may just do it tonight. That meant that Kim, Ted's wife would be upset with him again, but she would have to realize what being a cop's wife entailed. Just like a doctor, their time was not their own. The pay was lousy, but if she really knew Ted, she already knew that he wouldn't be happy doing anything else. He had seen many marriages in the department break up because of it. His first marriage was a case in point. He was young, ambitious and never home. He and his young bride became strangers living in the same house. After five years, there was nothing left so they divorced. He had loved her, but Larkin realized that he had loved his job more. Facing that reality, had kept him single all these years. He liked women: He just didn't like answering to anyone. When they began to get possessive, he moved on.

Cassie Thompson had dredged up feelings that came to the surface sometimes: the longing for female companionship; the notion that he was tired of being alone.

He hadn't realized until he pulled into her driveway how anxious he was to see her. "She may be involved in this up to her pretty little neck," he said aloud to himself. He needed to give himself the same pep talk he gave his men, the one about never becoming involved with a suspect. It made one unable to act and think clearly. All he could think of right now was being with her alone.

Her condominium was on the end with a little side yard and good-sized frontage. The upkeep was amazing. People in this neighborhood didn't mow their lawns, they manicured them. The landscaping was magazine perfect, the flowers mulched, and not a weed in sight.

There was no comparison to his little one-story ranch, which was overrun with weed and neglected shrubbery. He mentally told himself as he got out of his car, that it was just another reason why he and Cassie Thompson would not work. He couldn't afford her. The sinking feeling in the pit of his stomach should have jolted him back to reality, but it didn't.

Cassie Thompson took command of the room as she welcomed Larkin at the door, showing him into her spacious living quarters. It was luxurious, just like its owner.

Larkin had only interviewed her briefly, but he found her to be a very stimulating, beautiful, and intelligent woman. She was someone he wished he had met under different circumstances.

"Sorry to just drop in unannounced," he told her.

"I'm afraid I was warned that you were on your way, Mr. Larkin."

"I'm surprised you remembered my name." Now what caused him to say that?

"Frankly, it was Tina who remembered." A smile played around her bow-shaped lips. As if realizing he was staring at her mouth, she wet it with her tongue.

"Ahem—so she called you?"

"What she actually said was that Larkin was just here and he is on his way to see you. You know that old guy from yesterday."

"Old guy…" his eyebrows raised.

"She said you had to be at least fifty," she chuckled.

"She's not far off," he said, disgruntled. He must be slipping. No one had ever guessed him to more than forty. Sitting here with a beautiful woman and suddenly feeling over the hill wasn't a pleasant feeling.

"A very good-looking fifty, if you ask me." Her voice became low and husky.

Larkin looked up abruptly. The twinkle was back in her eyes and she was smiling. The woman like to shoot you down to watch you fall, and then pick you up again.

"Could I get you a drink?"

"I don't drink, but feel free if you'd like one yourself."

"I have beer," she offered, as though she thought it might make a difference.

She took a cigarette and offered him one. When he declined, she told him, "Could you be any more exciting Mr. Larkin?"

He watched her light up and thought to himself. *I must really be coming across as a stuffed shirt to this exciting woman.* Never had he felt more like a stick-in-the-mud.

"Most guys would be bending over backward trying to impress me by now. At least you're an original."

Larkin didn't know how to respond to that. He was well aware of the sexual tension in the room, but if she sensed it, she never let on.

This wasn't like him. He hadn't ever cared what a suspect's opinion of him was; and she was just another suspect. It didn't matter that the woman had gray-green eyes that seemed to change in different degrees of light; or that her lips begged him to kiss her. It didn't matter that she was witty, and sexy as hell, he told himself.

"What can I get for you then, Mr. Larkin? There has to be something I can offer you." There was, but he didn't want his face slapped.

"Actually there is something you can get me. How about a cup of coffee?" He could have bitten off his tongue after asking. The woman probably didn't own a maker let alone know how to make coffee.

"Great," she said, jumping to her feet. "You are human after all."

Larkin didn't figure her for the domestic type.

"Would you like cream, or sugar?" she called from her little kitchenette, that was visible from her living room.

"Cream only," he called back.

"All I have is creamer, I'm afraid."

"That's fine."

"You're more disciplined than me," she said loudly. "I load mine with cream and sugar."

A feeling pleasure welled inside of him knowing she was a coffee drinker.

She returned with the two steaming mugs, setting one in front of him, she handed him a napkin. When she accidentally touched his hand, something happened that he had always made fun of when he read it in books. Electricity charged up his arm and he almost dropped the napkin.

Larkin was relieved to see that the mugs were heavy ceramic instead of the delicate little tea cups he expected.

He took a long drink of his and told her, "You make a mean cup of brew, lady." He was impressed. He usually didn't care for other people's renditions.

"I learned from my dad," she said proudly.

"Are you a real coffee drinker, or do you just keep it around for your company?"

"I'm useless until after my second cup in the morning."

Larkin told himself he needed to get back to why he was here. It was just so good knowing there was something, no matter how small, that they shared in common.

"You are really close to your dad, aren't you?"

"Yes—I am. How about you, Mr. Larkin? Aren't you close to yours?"

"I can't say that I am. He wanted me to be a lawyer instead of a cop."

"That sounds like an insurmountable problem," she quipped.

The woman had a sarcastic, smart-ass attitude, but he liked her. He couldn't say why, he just did.

"What can I do for you Mr. Larkin?" she asked abruptly. "I know you just didn't come her to drink coffee."

"I just need some more information…"

"I'm afraid I told you everything I know about the situation the other day."

"There are some other things that have come up that I need to discuss with you."

"Sounds ominous," she said moving closer to him. She ground out her cigarette and sat up straighter in her chair. "What new information do you think I can give you?"

"I find it I interview people alone they're more honest about things."

"What you're trying to say is they tell you things they wouldn't say in front of someone close to them."

"I feel you would be careful to consider your father's and your siblings' feelings." He stared deeply into her eyes.

She took another cigarette from her case and asked him if he was sure he didn't want one. He assured her he didn't, but she could go ahead. She lit up, still glaring at him as if contemplating what she was about to say. She took a long draw and blew out the smoke.

"You're very observant, Mr. Larkin."

"Please call me Karl. 'Mr. Larkin' makes me feel as old as your sister thinks I am."

"Only if you call me Cassie," she said, sliding back in her seat.

"Is Cassie short for Cassandra?"

"No, actually my father insisted that I be named Cassie, not Cassandra."

"It fits you," he said, leaning back in his own chair.

"I noticed when you showed us your badge that your name is spelled with a K instead of C. I think that's pretty cool."

"That is about as exciting as my folks get, I'm afraid. They're pretty old-fashioned, and very conservative."

She took a long draw and exhaled the smoke. "There is something to be said for that these days. That's not such a bad thing, if you ask me."

Larkin was enjoying this interview a little too much. In the past, he had always made it a point not to mix business with pleasure.

"Let's get started, Cassie." He tried the name and liked the way sounded.

"Do me a favor," she said. "Don't ever call me Ms. Thompson, as you did the other day. I hate that."

"Deal," he said. He held out his hand and they shook on it.

"Okay, shoot the questions at me," she blurted.

"You do have a way with words, Cassie Thompson," he said, smiling at her.

"You have a way with the questions, Karl Larkin," she retaliated.

"Where were you during the time your mother went missing?"

"I would have been home in bed—and it's my stepmother."

"Was anyone with you?" Larkin wasn't sure he wanted to know the answer.

"Just me and Max."

"Is Max your boyfriend?" He knew she was divorced, and he found himself holding his breath waiting for her answer.

"My cat."

"I beg your pardon."

"Max is my cat. I'm surprised he hasn't been around to check you out."

"That's the one I never would have guessed," he said, staring at her. "I never figured you for a cat person."

"I suppose you think dogs are better?" She turned in her seat so she could see him better.

"Of course I do."

"You have one, don't you," she accused.

"His name is Ho Bo. He's just a stray mutt. He came to my door one night in the dead of winter. It was snowy and freezing outside, and he was all wet and shivering. He reminded me of myself, so, I kept him. They say dogs are a man's best friend, you know."

"I do believe you have a human side, Karl Larkin. Who would have guessed?" A little half smile crossed her lips.

"As for dogs, you can always trust them to be faithful," he told her. He was uncomfortable with the conversation becoming too personal.

"The reason men like dogs is because they will take any abuse and come running back for more. Men like their own women to be the same. Cats don't suck up."

"What are you saying?"

"I'm saying you can beat a dog, talk mean to it and call it five minutes later and it will come running to you wagging its tail and slobbering all over you. You do that to a cat, and call them; they will take your number and get back to you."

Karl laughed aloud. *It was a nice sound*, Cassie thought. *She liked it a lot. He was a little uptight for her taste, but he didn't look, or act, like a cop.*

"How did you and your mother get along?" The question came abruptly.

Now he was acting like a cop. "She was my stepmother, and we didn't."

"Care to elaborate?"

"What can I say? We had little to do with each other. She married my dad too soon after my mother's death. My dad worked a lot, the rest of the time he was busy with her. I felt abandoned." As she talked, her sadness showed. "Thank God, they left me with my grandparents. I would have been miserable living with her."

"Would you say you dislike her?"

"There are different degrees or dislike, Karl. What do you want me to say? Did I hate her? Yes. Did I hate her enough to kill her? Probably? Did I kill her? The answer is no, but you don't know if you believe that, do you, Detective?"

Karl didn't answer and she continued, "Why don't you have a little notepad like your buddy?"

"I don't need one. I have an excellent memory—a photographic one, they tell me. Cramer takes notes, and I go over it, and from then on it's right here in my computer," he pointed to his head.

"Get out."

"It's true."

"And you are wasting...."

"My potential. Now you sound like my parents."

Cassie grew quiet, for she had hit a nerve.

"Why did you hate her?"

"I hated her because of the way she treated my dad."

"Could you tell me a little about her character, I mean."

"What character?" Cassie laughed, but there was no amusement in it. "You want me to tell you what she was like."

"If you would."

"She was a paranoid, insecure, jealous freak. My dad has been cleaning up her messes for years."

She started to light another cigarette but decided against it. Larkin knew by her reaction that her stepmother was a sore subject.

"What kind of messes are you talking about?"

"I'd rather not say. It would only hurt my dad if he knew that I was discussing his personal life."

"Is there anything you can tell me? The more I know the easier it will be for me to clear this up."

"She would follow my dad around trying to catch him having an affair. She was always accusing him of that. What I hated most is she would drag one of the kids with her. She was always trying to prove it to them. Dad told you about his secretary. There was no reason for her to drag Tina along for that."

"Is there any chance that it might have been true that your dad was having an affair?" Seeing the look in her face, he bent forward and touched her arm. "I have to ask these things. I'm sorry."

"I know it's your job. I understand that. But the answer is no; he wasn't."

"I have something I really don't know how to ask you…"

"Go ahead. I'll answer if I can."

"Do you remember us taking DNA from everyone?"

"Yes."

"There is no easy way to say this, but you are the only one of the children who could belong to your father."

The shock showed on her face.

"You didn't know, did you?"

"No—but it doesn't really surprise me," she said at last. "I could have added 'whore' to that list I gave you, but I was trying to be nice."

"I have found when one partner is suspicious of the other; it's usually because they're the one having the affair."

She nodded her head.

"Do you think your father knew the kids didn't belong to him?"

"I have no idea. He never mentioned it to me if he did."

"Do you think he would have stayed with her if he had known?"

She thought about it for a time before she answered, "He probably would have. She has done some rotten things to him and he always blames it on her childhood."

"Some people overcome their childhood," Larkin blurted.

"Exactly," she agreed. "Not many of us have lived the Brady Bunch life."

"I know she was sexually abused," Larkin said.

"My dad didn't discuss it with me. The only thing he said was, their father had abused Carrie and Julie both. Neither woman mentioned their past, or living in the hills of the North Carolina. I found it odd that they never talked about relatives."

"Do you think her murder might have something to do with her past?"

"It could, I guess." Cassie looked thoughtful. "But you heard her sister. She has set up other little dramas in the past…"

"There's one difference," Larkin reminded. "This one got her killed."

"I knew she was capable of it," Cassie breathed.

Larkin nodded his head.

"I knew she was capable of it," Cassie said. "How did it go wrong?"

"What we're thinking right now is she hired someone willing to do the fake kidnapping. We really don't know what went wrong. Maybe she refused to give him the money, or maybe he wanted it all. Whatever happened, he wound up killing her. She had Tina deliver the note for her. She went to all the trouble of getting the guy to do the note and even sealing the envelope so his DNA would be on it."

"That's Julie. She was thorough."

"I have to admit it shows a pretty devious mind," Larkin agreed. "Do you think any of the servants would have helped her with a scheme like this?"

"I don't think so. Not one of them liked her."

"That's all the more reason to kill her."

"They are loyal to my dad. They wouldn't do it." Cassie was vehement.

"She might have threatened their jobs."

"I never thought of that. It never hurt her to drag my..." She started to say Julie brought her sister and brother into her plots, but changed what she was about to say. They were not really her sister and brother, and it hurt because she loved them.

"You're not going to tell them that Dad isn't their father, are you?"

"Oh no. There's no need to tell them as far as I'm concerned."

Cassie relaxed, breathing a sigh of relief.

"Your father knew about Todd," Larkin said. "He knew that he belonged to Julie's own father. She had an affair soon after they were married, so he wasn't sure about Tina."

"I know the woman was abused, but my father gave her everything. I'm sorry, Karl, but I can't seem to muster any sympathy for the woman. I'm glad she's dead. Now maybe my father can have some kind of a life."

Larkin made no comment, only took another drink of his coffee. He was glad Cramer didn't hear this. They were silent for a time, each with their own thoughts.

"Thanks for being honest with me about the kids," Cassie said at last.

"Sometimes honesty is not a good thing," Larkin said.

She reached forward and put a hand on his arm. Again, Karl felt the reaction. "You will find, Karl, that I prefer the truth, even if it's painful."

"I believe that," he said, studying her. "I will be as forthcoming with you as I can without jeopardizing the case. I promise." He made the cross-your-heart sign.

"I couldn't ask for more."

"Do you think your father will tell Tina and Todd?"

"Not on your life," Cassie blurted. "Dad may be guilty of neglecting his children, but he would never intentionally hurt one of us. He is a good man, Karl."

Larkin would reserve judgement for the present, but he also knew that Cassie believed it with her whole heart.

"Is he a suspect in the case? I have always heard that the spouse is the first one they look at." She was studying his face intently.

Larkin knew she needed reassurance that her dad was not a suspect, but he couldn't put her mind at ease. Staring at the scared look on her face, he wanted to hold her. He was doing something he had always warned the people who worked for him not to do. He was getting personally involved with the family he was investigating, or at least one of them.

"I'm afraid that everyone is a suspect at this point." He hoped to sidestep the question.

"Even me—right?"

He nodded his head and she gave him a little half-hearted smile. "Once a cop always, a cop, I guess."

"I'm afraid so," he agreed, bringing them both back to reality.

"What comes next?" She seemed to brace herself.

"More unpleasantness, I'm afraid. One thing we're doing is tracing the money…"

"Yes?"

"There is just no easy way to put this."

"Go on." Her eyes hardened slightly.

"My partner said there was a large deposit made to your account around the time your step-mother came up missing."

"And you want to know if I am slimy enough to extort half a million dollars from my dad."

"I have to pursue every lead. I'm sorry."

"Of course you do." She smiled, but it didn't reach her eyes. "The money is from my job."

"Are you saying that the money is from your publisher?"

"Bingo, you win the prize."

"I had no idea that…"

"That writing stupid little romances paid so well." Her eyes were flashing fire.

That was exactly what he was thinking, but he wasn't going to admit it in the mood she was in.

"You know, Mr. Larkin, I meet hundreds of people every year that are just like you. I want you to think about something. Most people desperately want and need love, even if they never admit it."

"I—I guess you're right…"

"Quick—Mr. Larkin—what kind of songs do you think jam the airwaves?"

"Love songs, I guess."

"You're damn right. People pay thousands of dollars to dating services, looking for Mr. or Ms. Right. Why? Because they're looking for love."

"You've made your point."

"Then there are the movies. In every kind of movie there is an underlying love story. I think I'm safe in saying that love is a big business."

"I never thought of it like that, I guess," Karl admitted.

"No, you didn't, Mr. Larkin, because you're ignorant of the writing business. Did you know that statistics say romances generate about a billion dollars a year?"

"No, I didn't."

"Did you know that over fifty percent of all paperback fiction sold are romances? In any given year there are a couple thousand romances written and released. People gobble them up and publishers know it. Some lucky writers have honed their writing to a fine art and come up with million-dollar contracts. The money in question is what is known as an advance against royalties, Mr. Larkin."

"I thought we had decided on first names," he reminded.

"I'm sorry, Mr. Larkin, but it doesn't seem so friendly and informal anymore."

"I plead ignorance, Cassie. I truly didn't mean to insult your craft. I rarely come in contact with writers, romantic or any other kind."

"The truth is, Mr. Larkin, the writers of romantic fiction are some of the best writers in the world."

"I will have to take your word for that. But I am a police officer and you are probably ignorant about what I do…"

She laughed. "I probably know more than you think, Karl. We call it research."

"You mean you do research for a love story?" The words were out before he could swallow them back.

"You just don't get it, do you, Larkin?" she snapped. "If I don't know the first thing about fishing—and I don't—if I have my hero fly-fishing for perch and you really use a stringer, some sports nut who knows nothing else will call me on it. Trust me, it happened."

"You're kidding."

"It's happened to me more than once."

"I really never knew how much work was involved," he said.

"You're just like most people," she said. "You think all a writer has to do is tell a few lies, write them down on paper and get paid for it?"

He wasn't about to admit that, but that was pretty much what he thought. "Can we call a truce? People's feelings get in the way sometimes, while I'm doing my job. I can't help that."

"Anyway if you had talked to your buddy again you would have known that when the bank learned that the police were inquiring about my finances, they called me. I gave permission for him to go over my records."

"I appreciate your cooperation."

"Don't. If I refused, I knew you would just get a court order, and I have nothing to hide."

She offered him her hand. "Truce it is," she said.

He reached out to take her hand, definitely knowing he enjoyed it too much. She was right about everyone wanting and needing love. She was an intelligent lady, and a very dangerous adversary to his heart.

Larkin realized that it was almost quitting time and there was no way he would be able to make it back in time to talk to Ted. He wasn't going to call him and tell him to wait; they would just have to go over what they had learned the next day. He had enjoyed the conversation so much he had forgotten the time. He could never remember doing that before.

He checked his watch. "I'm going to have to go. This has been an enjoyable afternoon and I hate to bring it to a close..."

"It's been enlightening for me also," she said. "I think I just might make my next hero a cop." She had walked him to the door and they were standing face to face. They were much too close for him to remain unaffected.

"Would you be interested in renewing this conversation over dinner sometime?" He tried to stop himself, but it was as if his tongue had a mind of its own.

"I might be," she replied huskily. "I have to do research for my new book."

"So, you mean to make it business, and not personal."

"It's up to you," she said very close to his mouth. Her lips were so full and luscious, and so near. All he would have to do is move a few inches and...

Her phone rang. Larkin cursed it under his breath, and yet thought of it as his savior.

"That was my editor," she explained. "She wants seven chapters by next week. I will be up all night tonight," she sighed. "Now about that dinner..."

"I was thinking about this Saturday, but it sounds like you'll be busy."

"What's the matter, Detective, are you getting cold feet?"

The phone call had bought him back to reality. He should be backpedaling out of this, but instead he heard himself saying, "I have Saturday off, how about I pick you up around seven o'clock."

"That sounds great. Where are we going?"

"I'll call you Friday and we'll decide."

"That's great. After working all week I'll be ready."

CHAPTER 7

---◆---

Larkin could hardly wait until Friday evening to call Cassie. He didn't want to appear too anxious, but it was all he had thought of all week. He hadn't heard from her since Tuesday at her apartment and just prayed she would be home to take his call. She picked up the receiver on the second ring.

"Hello." The simple answering of her phone sent a thrill through him.

"It's Karl..."

"Karl who?"

"You know...Detective Larkin."

There was a pause and then she gave a husky little laugh. "I knew who you were; I was just messing with you. Lighten up a little, Karl."

With anyone else his impatience would have shown through, but he was just relieved she was still talking to him after the comments he made about her work.

"Are we still on for tomorrow night?"

That was just the cop in him, Cassie decided—all business.

"Sure. I have been saving up my appetite all week."

"What sounds good for dinner?"

"I'm thinking steak," she said quickly.

"That sounds wonderful," Larkin blurted. "I was about halfway afraid you were a vegetarian."

"Do I look like a vegetarian? I'm strictly a meat-and-potatoes girl."

"I didn't know. You being a cat person and all," he kidded.

"You goof. If I don't get off this phone, I'm going to be writing this weekend instead of eating. Where would you like to eat?"

He had a horror of her choosing some fancy place where it would take a month's salary to afford. "Do you like Rogers Steak House?"

"It's my favorite."

"You've got it," he said, relieved. "I'll pick you up at seven o'clock."

Larkin and Cassie arrived at the restaurant about seven-thirty. Being with her was a bittersweet for Larkin, who knew he needed to keep their relationship on a professional level. He had enjoyed the afternoon he spent with her so much—even when she was angry with him, he felt so alive. Besides, he told himself, if cops couldn't date someone they met investigating a crime they would never find time for socializing.

He should have called and cancelled the date and he decided that after tonight he would cool it. It just wasn't right dating someone involved in a murder case. He had to be honest with himself; he was falling in love with someone who might be capable of murder. She had said she hated her stepmother, and that she was glad she was dead. Those were strong words.

There was a battle going inside. He knew he should be giving that case his full attention, and all he could think about was Cassie.

They talked away the evening and Larkin was surprised at how hard her job really was. He was amazed that when a book was finished, there were rewrites to do, and deadlines to meet. She had to worry about plot, viewpoint, and pace, whatever that was. Just hearing about it made his head spin. What surprised him the most was that he was actually interested in what she did.

He shared with her what it was like to be a detective and be involved with the lower side of human nature. He shared with her how frustrating it was collecting evidence that wouldn't hold up in court. He told her how angry he felt when a judge let someone he knew was guilty back on the streets. He knew it wouldn't be long before the police were hunting them again. He told her about the case of a small girl that had bothered him the most. They never identified the child. She was buried in an unmarked grave, which he and other officers paid for. Larkin could count the unsolved cases on one hand, but her death never allowed him to rest.

"The unsolved ones are called cold cases, aren't they?" Cassie asked.

"That's what most people call them."

"What do you call them?" She stared at him intently.

"I don't label them," he said, squirming under her scrutiny. "I go over them every time we slow down. Sometimes I get lucky and find the right clue. I'm proud to say we have very few unsolved cases in our precinct."

"It sounds like a very difficult job," she said at last.

"It is—but it's one I chose for myself, and I can't see doing any other."

"To thine own self be true."

"Something like that," he agreed.

"Writing is the same for me. My dad jokes about all the scribbled pieces of paper he found all over the house when I was growing up."

"I'm amazed it's such hard work."

"It's not glamorous as some people believe. I have to work hard so my reader doesn't have to. When they buy a book, they want to be entertained, not stumble around trying to decipher my meaning."

"I get it," Larkin told her. "Your writing is not fun for you; you have to make it entertaining for your reader."

"You learn slow, Detective, but you learn well," she chuckled.

"Don't get me wrong. I paint pictures with words and nothing gives me greater pleasure than having a fan tell me they couldn't put my book down. That is when I know I've done my job well. When does it happen for you…? I mean, when do you know you have done your job?"

Larkin thought for a second. "Every time I look into the face of a victim, I make a silent vow to avenge them. My job is done when I bring their murderer to justice."

"How do you feel if you can't find their killer?"

"I feel frustrated, with any unfinished business," Karl admitted.

"How do you feel about Julie's case?" she asked suddenly.

"The same as I feel about any other," he was honest. He hoped she didn't think her opinion of the woman would influence the way he conducted his case. Julie had been a beautiful woman, and staring into her lifeless face, he had made her the silent promise he made to every murdered victim. He would not stop until justice was done. "I plan on finding her killer."

"I respect that, Karl. But do you believe in mitigating circumstances...?"

"If you are asking me if I feel there is ever an excuse for murder, the answer is no."

"No matter how rotten a person is...?"

"I'm afraid I have to disagree with you, Karl."

"And who is to say when a person crosses the line and no longer deserves to live?" His voice rose slightly.

"Are you telling me that you have gone through how many years...?"

"Forty-eight..." he supplied.

"Don't tell me, you have never come across someone you'd like to kill... Never investigated someone you thought got what they deserved."

"Yes—I can say that. I was always taught that life is precious,"

"I don't believe you." She took a drink of her beer.

"We all have enemies, I'm not denying that," Larksin said. "But not everyone kills."

"You must be far nobler than me, because I have fantasized about killing Julie."

"You hated her that much?" Larkin frowned. He didn't like hearing this. He was much too fond of her to want to think of her as a suspect.

"As far as I concerned—that woman ruined my father's life and she deserved to die. That's the way I feel, and I can't help it."

The conversation was unsettling. He knew he needed to steer away from the case altogether. "Tell me about your childhood," he said at last.

"There isn't a lot to tell. My mother died of cancer when I was four. Dad threw himself into his work, and my grandparents took care of me. I didn't have much of a childhood, really."

Thus, the remark she had made to him earlier about her father neglecting his children, but never hurting then intentionally.

"So, your childhood wasn't exactly a happy one."

"How about you, Karl? I seem to remember you saying that yours wasn't so great either."

Maybe there wasn't a safe subject with her, he thought. "I told you I was skinny and nerdy, and always being put down. My parents were very strict and controlling, and they were determined that I was going to college and become a lawyer. I was just a determined not to."

"Did you rebel just because it was what they wanted?"

"Not entirely. But I guess it made me even more determined to do things my way."

"What about sister and brothers?"

"I was an only child, born late in my mother's life. By the time I came along they had given up hopes of having children, and here I was. They had spent thirty years planning my future before I got here. I'm a major disappointment to them, I'm afraid."

"Just because you wanted to be a cop, instead of a lawyer."

"They're pretty set in their ways. With them, there is not much gray area. Everything is either black or white, if you know what I mean."

"I've known people like that," Cassie said.

"When I went into the police academy they had a fit, and little by little we just stopped the visits and phone calls. Oh, I've tried to get together with them a few times, but things are always awkward. I finally just gave up and got on with my life."

"Do you miss them?"

"Are you studying to be a detective, Mrs. Thompson?"

"I'm sorry, Karl, but I'm curious about what makes you tick."

"I do miss them, but I can't live my life to please them. It's a bad situation."

Cassie Thompson was a fascinating woman. Not only was she physically attractive, she was intelligent and well versed on many subjects. It was probably all the research she had to do for her profession. Karl knew he ought to call it a night, but found it hard to leave her.

"I've enjoyed tonight so much," he told her, "but Ted is coming over tomorrow…"

"Will you two go over the case?"

"Yes, but it's like Cramer says; the more we find out the less we know. That probably doesn't make sense to you." He smiled.

"Maybe I've been around you too long, but it does," she laughed. "Am I a suspect?" The question was blunt.

"Everyone is a suspect at this point." Karl was honest with her.

"You know that it's never the most likely person."

"I'm afraid that's only in the movies," he said, smiling. "I've found that more times than not, it's the person with the strongest motive." Karl stopped, for in this case it seemed to be her.

"Was this date business or pleasure?"

"Believe me, it was not business. You're a very beautiful, interesting woman and I enjoyed being with you. I've tried not to bring business into it."

"You did well, Karl." She bent forward, looking into his eyes. "I was afraid you would spend the evening grilling me about my family. I have enjoyed myself as well."

"Maybe we could do it again sometime."

"I'd like that." She smiled.

"It's hard to say when I'll find the time…"

"Do you think you're making progress with the case?" she asked abruptly.

"Note that you're the one bringing it up, lady."

"I just want it over because of my dad."

"We have DNA from the envelope—I suppose you knew that?"

"My dad did mention it to me. Have you found out who it belongs to?"

"That's the thing. It would be such a break in the case if we could."

"Who have you tested?"

"We tested all of the family, every employee, even the people who work for and with your dad. There are no matches. We have even taken samples from Tina's boyfriend and Todd's best friend, Kyle. We're still awaiting the results on them."

"What you need to do is start tracing the people my stepmother hung out with." Cassie's remark was bitter.

"That has been Ted's job all week. He has been trying to find out if she was having an affair."

"You mean finding out about her latest affair." Cassie sniffed.

"A penny for your thoughts," Cassie said at last. "I could see the wheels turning in your brain."

"I thought you were going to say you smelled wood burning."

"There's no wood there," she said, taking her finger and playfully poking his forehead. "You're a very intelligent man, very observant, and have a photographic memory besides. It has to be priceless in your profession."

"It is."

"I think it would be invaluable in any profession. I sure wish I had it."

"It helps when people tell me the truth," Karl said.

"But if they lie, you know it, right?"

"Has anyone lied to you in this case?"

"I don't know." He had to laugh at her exuberance. "If they have I haven't caught them yet. I have a good memory, but I'm not psychic."

She laughed at herself. "I am just so fascinated that someone has that good of a memory."

"It was when I was in school that I found out. I could read the material for a test, and visualize it just like in the book. I would write it down word for word, and my teacher would accuse me of cheating. When I explained how I could see it in my mind, he didn't believe me. He made me study this long list of numbers then he tested me. When I got them all right, he made me do it several more times before he was convinced."

"That is so awesome. You're incredible."

Her words gave Larkin a rush of pleasure. He wasn't accustomed to compliments. Even his folks had always made him feel like he didn't quite measure up. His teachers let him know he was wasting his potential. His young wife had been more interested in her own needs.

"You're giving me the big head," he said at last.

"You could have done anything in life, but you chose to go against everyone and be a detective. Could I ask you what drove you?"

He had to think for a moment before he could put it into words.

"I told you I was a little scrawny kid when I was growing up. I didn't feel that I could fight my way out of a wet paper bag. One day on the bus, the school bully started beating up this nerdy guy in front of me. He pounded the crap out of him and no one raised a finger to help him. Many of other kids egged him on and it just seemed so unfair. I told myself right then: I was going to be someone with authority and I would stand up for the people like him."

"You were determined to right the wrongs of the world."

"I guess that was the idea."

"The desire is just as strong today, isn't it?"

"Yes, I guess it is."

"That's very noble, Detective, but does it always work?"

"More times than not, I'd have to say."

"Only because you're the kind of man who will take a stand."

"I will take that as compliment," he said at last.

"It was meant as one." Her eyes softened as she stared at him in the dim light, and a country love song crooned softly in the background.

"You remind me a lot of my father."

Larkin didn't know how to respond to that. Did she think of him as a father figure, or did she see him as having the same qualities? Frankly, he was afraid to ask.

When he only stared as if trying to figure her out she said, "That is about as high of a compliment as I can give. My father believes in fair play too, though it usually turns and bites him in the butt."

"I've had it happen a few times also," he said.

Cassie looked at her own watch. "I need to go also. I still have some work on those last chapters."

"Can I call you tomorrow?"

"I won't be home. I'm spending Sunday with my family. I'm sorry."

"Don't be," he reassured her. "Family is important." As he made the statement, he realized how much he did miss his mom and dad. He just wished things could be different.

"I will call you sometime this weekend," he said as he helped her from the car.

At her door, he bent to give her a slight kiss he felt appropriate for a first date. Instead, she pulled his head down to hers for a deep searching kiss that he felt clear to his toes. She let him go, smiled and went inside.

CHAPTER 8

———— ◆ ————

Monday morning Ted and Karl went to interview the Risners. Karl called his colleague the night before and told him not to come over Sunday as planned. He had spent a late night with Cassie Thompson, which he failed to mention, and he needed to sleep in.

"What do we know about these people?" Ted asked, as they drove along.

"Not much, really. Just that she's Julie Cromwell's sister and James is her husband. Didn't you think it was interesting their boy Toby was a visitor to the Cromwell's place on Saturday before Cromwell found the note?"

"Do you think he delivered the ransom note? I thought Tina said her mother gave her the note."

"What if it's not true? Tina knew about her mother's scheme. What if she and Toby hatched a plan of their own? Toby fixes the note and delivers it to Tina. She puts it were her dad can find it."

"That completely throws a monkey wrench in the works to think that Julie Cromwell might not have hired the person who killed her," Cramer said.

"We know she didn't do the note. Someone licked that envelope whose DNA we have yet to determine. Someone who the guards would never suspect either gave it to Julie Cromwell, or delivered it to an unknown person at that house. If it didn't happen like Tina claims, we need to know who both of those people are."

"Do we have this Toby's DNA?"

"When I called and told the Risners we were coming, I asked for him to be available for testing."

"Won't he be in school?"

"This is spring break."

"Did we get back the results on Tina's friend, Snake, and Todd's friend, Kyle?"

"No—I guess I'll have to start looking over Blake's shoulder again. There still hasn't been a hit running the mysterious guy's DNA through CODIS either."

"You would think a person involved something like this would have left fingerprints. I'm sure he has been in trouble before," Ted remarked. "This case is so damn frustrating. Every time we get a good lead, it just fizzles out."

"It's one of those cases, hopefully, that comes together all at once."

"We seem to have too many suspects, and we can't eliminate anyone."

"This is it," Larkin said. He and Ted were cruising a ritzy new housing addition on the outskirts of town. The house was a large ranch with wings built at each end. Larkin looked over the yard, which he assumed was two lots, compared to the others in the development. It wasn't a mansion like the Cromwell's, but it had set the owners back a buck or two.

"Nice house," Cramer said as he drew his long frame out of the car.

"Beats the hell out of anything you and I will ever afford," Larkin said.

Carrie let them in. She looked to have lost as much sleep as he had, Larkin thought. She was tall and gaunt with black circles under her eyes. Her dark hair was shoulder length and straight, her eyes slightly receding. It was easy to see that her sister had gotten the looks in the family.

Her husband, James, was waiting for them in the living room. Larkin and Ted both received a nod from him in acknowledgement "Would you sit down," the greeting from Carrie was stiff and formal.

Ted took a set and commented on the weather. Mrs. Risner bluntly ask him to forego the small talk and get on with it, because she and James needed to get back to work.

"Sure," Larkin leaned forward to see them both better. "What is your occupation, Mrs. Risner?"

"I'm in charge of the welfare department here in town. My department deals with child abuse and domestic violence."

Larkin thought about her past. It probably was a factor in her choice of career.

"That's a noble profession, Mrs. Risner. You must find helping people a rewarding experience?"

"Yes—thanks," she softened a little. "Sometimes it's difficult for me the way the children are treated."

Now Larkin was sure she was reliving scenes from her own past.

"Did you and your sister get along well?"

She squirmed in her seat, flashing a look at her husband. "We weren't that close. We never socialized, Mr. Larkin. My sister was pretty self-involved. She never believed anyone had problems, but her. She was always mixed up in one of her little dramas, while her husband and children went to hell in a handbasket."

"So you thought she neglected her family?"

"Let me put it this way, Mr. Larkin. She only thought about herself and what she wanted."

"That doesn't tell me how you felt about her."

"I didn't like my sister. Is that what you want to hear?"

"Only if that is true."

"She was my sister. Of course, I loved her. I just never cared for the way she treated people."

"Including the way she treated you?"

"She acted like she was better than us."

"What about you, James? Did you like your sister-in-law?"

"I can't say that I did."

"And why is that?"

"It's like my wife said. She was a selfish woman."

"So, am I am safe in saying that neither of you cared for her?"

Carrie was visually flustered. "We didn't kill her, Mr. Larkin—if that is what you're implying."

"I notice you don't live very far from the Cromwells."

"We live close, but we socialized very little," James volunteered again. Carrie flashed him a quick look as if warning him to be careful.

"Actually, Toby and the children are closer than any of the grownups. He and Todd are close in age, I suppose that's why."

Larkin watched Carrie's face change as she talked about her Toby. There was no mistaking; he was the apple of her eye.

"Toby is very fond of his Uncle Lawrence also. They share some of the same interests."

Again, she gave Larkin the impression she had feelings for Lawrence.

He looked toward James. He acted uncomfortable with the turn the conversation had taken.

"Speaking of Toby," Larkin said. "Can we take a DNA sample now?"

Carrie's jaw visually tightened, as she told him, "He's not here."

"Where is he?" He had made a point of asking her to have him available. He hated someone disobeying a direct order, even if she were a civilian.

"He's in Florida on spring break. He had a chance to go with his friends, and the boy works hard in school. He deserves this. He can give a sample some other time."

Larkin was angry. He would get the sample, even if it meant a court order. Her sending Toby out of town might delay it, but it wouldn't stop him. He figured while he was still angry might be a good time to plunge right in asking James about the money.

"Mr. Risner, it's come to our attention that you deposited a substantial amount into your account a day or two after the kidnapping."

"What!" Carrie exclaimed. "You're snooping around in our finances. You have some nerve. Don't tell him a thing, James," she sputtered.

"All he has to do is see the judge, Carrie, and he will allow it." James seemed resigned to the fact. "If you must know, our company received a huge contract to build a new strip mall just west of the town. The money was the first draw to start the project."

"We might not have as much money as the Cromwells," Carrie ground out, "but we aren't destitute either."

It was easy to see there was jealousy between the two families.

"I'm sorry, but we have to find out who killed your sister, Mrs. Risner. One way of doing that is to find the money extorted from Lawrence Cromwell. I believe there was someone inside the circle of family and friends who assisted an unknown assailant in the kidnapping and murder."

"Why do you believe it was some insider?" Carrie snapped.

"Someone other than your sister fixed that note, and it was delivered without the guards getting suspicious. It had to be someone the guards would allow in without question. Did you know your son, Toby, was a visitor to the Cromwell estate Saturday afternoon, the day before Cromwell received the note?"

"Are—are you accusing Toby…"

"I'm not accusing anyone, Mrs. Risner, but you can rest assured I will check out every lead."

"I'm outraged that we're being harassed like this," she sniffed.

"Ma'am," Cramer broke in, "we are not here to harass anyone. I'm sorry you feel this way."

"Mr. Risner, will you be willing to call your bank and give them the okay for us to confirm the information you gave us?" Larkin asked.

"I'll do better than that. I will go by the bank with you and tell them you have my permission to go over the records."

"I appreciate your cooperation."

"I just hope this mess can be cleared up soon," Risner said.

"I bet you find that my sister planned the whole thing and probably refused to pay the slime ball she hired to help her. He probably became angry and killed her."

"If that is what happened. Do you have any idea who she would have gotten to go along with a plan like that?"

"How would I know?" She looked up at him quickly. "I told you we never traveled in the same circles."

"I really hate to ask you these personal questions, Mrs. Risner, but there is an aspect of the case we haven't explored yet."

"What do you mean, Detective?"

"What I'm saying is that everyone is assuming it's all about the money. What if there is another motive?"

"What other motive could there possibly be, Detective?" She gave a nervous little laugh. "It's all about greed."

"Do you think it could be someone connected to her past?" Larkin tried to be delicate in the way he approached the subject.

Carrie turned pale and squirmed in her seat. She visually braced herself.

"I have been told that you and your sister were both victims of child abuse."

"I am not talking about this." She jumped from her seat and began to pacing back and forth wringing her hands.

"Mrs. Risner—there is nothing for you to be ashamed of. It wasn't your fault..."

"Then why, Mr. Larkin, do I feel such humiliation when people dredge it up?" Her eyes glazed over as she spoke. "People just keep probing and picking and sticking their noses where they don't belong. Why can't I just be allowed to forget?"

"All right, Mrs. Risner," he said at last. "We will let it go for now. If you can think of anyone from the past who would want to hurt your sister, please let me know. Something you ought to keep in mind though—if it is someone from the past, they might want to harm you, also."

Carrie was holding her head and frowning. James came over to stand beside her, putting his arm and her shoulders. "Is it a migraine?" he asked, his forehead furrowing into a frown. "I'll get your medicine." He was back in a few minutes with a couple of pills and a glass of water.

"How much more do we have here?" he asked. "My wife needs to lie down."

"You may go if you like, Mrs. Risner. Your husband can finish up."

Without saying another word, she hurried from the room, calling back over her shoulder for James to call her work.

After she closed the door to the bathroom, James told them, "I'm sorry but my wife is high-strung. She's easily upset and when she gets agitated it brings on one of her headaches."

He rung his hands as if he too were upset, but Larkin thought it had more to do with the mood with his wife was in the questioning.

"Who mentioned the abuse to you?" James had moved into the chair his wife had vacated and lowered his voice.

"Lawrence Cromwell spoke briefly to me about it. He said in respect to his wife he wouldn't go into detail. His wife was much like your own, and didn't wish to talk about it."

James seemed relieved but nodded his head, agreeing with Cromwell that it was a painful subject for both women.

"Could you tell us something about your wife's childhood, Mr. Risner?"

"I don't know anything, Mr. Larkin. Carrie would never discuss it with me. You know how most people will remember things that bring back memories. It's like my brother did this, or my father said that."

Larkin shook his head, and James continued, "Carrie never does that. It's as if she has erased it from her mind. When we first met I used to try to get her to talk, but the way she reacted, it didn't take me long to learn to stay clear of the subject."

"She never told you anything?" Larkin found that hard to believe. "If that's the case, how did you know she was abused?"

"Larry told me also. He didn't dwell on it. He just said that their father had abused both Carrie and Julie. He implied that it was more than just sexual abuse. He said it was physical and emotional as well."

"Damn," Larkin swore.

That was an ultimate betrayal of a parent, and really explained a lot about both women's behavior.

"I'm sorry to bring up such hurt for your wife." Larkin meant what he said. "I think we need to wrap this up. We can go to the bank now and, Mr. Risner, I still need your son's DNA."

James said they could call and set up a time for Toby to be there, and Cramer and Larkin waited for him at the front door while he checked on his wife.

James assured the bank it was okay for the police to look over a printout of his finances and he went back to his construction crew. It took a short time to confirm what James had told them was true, and the money trail grew cold once again.

CHAPTER 9

———— ♦ ————

B ack at the office, Larkin had to force himself to concentrate on the case. Even the two cups of coffee wasn't helping. Ted had gone after his usual box of rolls even though it was almost lunch, and Larkin could have hugged him when he showed up, because things, on the surface, were back to normal.

"So what did you find out about the kids?" Ted was talking with his mouth full, but today it seemed less irritating.

"Cromwell knew Todd wasn't his, but he didn't know about Tina."

"Ouch." Ted winced.

"It didn't seem to be a big shock to him, however."

"Did he know who Todd's father was?"

"Yes. That is the main reason he wanted her out of her father's home."

"Do you think the murderer could be someone Julie Cromwell was involved with?"

"It could be a former lover," Larkin said. "It would be easy to help her with a scheme like this. How are you coming with that anyway?"

"She seems to have cleaned up her act lately. I talked to the servants, and the guards. She didn't work outside the home. If she did have a boyfriend, no one knew about him."

"The guards said she never went out late at night?"

"Mrs. White says she was too busy watching Lawrence to have an affair of her own. She also said that most men would have dumped her years ago."

"She wasn't well liked," Larkin admitted, "but she still has a right for justice."

"It was just as we thought. Tina confessed to putting the letter there. Her mother gave her the note, and told her where to put it. She was under the impression they were going to teach her father a lesson. Mrs. Cromwell promised to buy the girl an expensive dress for a school dance, if she did it."

"Oh, a mother's love," Ted mocked. "The woman was a piece of work."

"I can only imagine the things in her past that made her that way," Larkin said.

"Don't tell me you' re excusing her like Cromwell does?"

"No, but the environment you're raised in has an impact on your life. You saw Carrie Risner's reaction when I mentioned their past."

"What does Cromwell think about Tina not being his?"

"He says it makes no difference; she's still his daughter."

"I think he is too good to be true."

"He said he forgave his wife because he loves her. He believes that all her problems stem from her childhood." It even sounded lame to Karl when he spoke it aloud, but since he had met Cassie Thompson, he could better understand Cromwell's feelings.

"What about the Risners?"

"I think the broad is crazy," Ted confessed. "And her old man is scared of his own shadow."

"I think I need to study about effects of sexual abuse," Karl said. "I can't get over the gut feeling that it has something to do with Julie's murder."

Ted stared at him but didn't comment. He knew better than to go against his boss's gut feelings.

"What did you find out about the kids?"

"I confronted them about sneaking out and they admitted it."

"Did they say where they went?"

"The Paris Club-do you know it?"

"Only by reputation. It's a popular teen hangout in the area. They serve nonalcoholic mixed drinks, but that is debatable. I've heard they don't serve alcohol, but they tend to look the other way if the kids spike their own."

"I've heard that as well."

"Tina sneaked out to meet her boyfriend, Snake. By the way, we have another suspect."

"Snake?" Cramer raised his eyebrows. He had finished off three rolls, and to Karl's relief pushed the box aside.

"I don't know what kind, but yes, it's Snake. He has a record; petty crime stuff, I'm told."

"Do you think he might have graduated?"

"It's been known to happen," Karl agreed. "We can't take anything at face value in this case. A million dollars is a great incentive to go beyond the usual."

"What do we know for sure?" Cramer asked.

"We know that Julie Cromwell was shot and we have the weapon used. We know it's murder and not suicide. Her murderer faced her and shot her while she stood on the deck. The killer shot her through the heart, she fell, and he walked closer and put a bullet through her brain. Then he threw the gun into the lake, followed by the victim's body. There were no fingerprints found on the gun. We don't know if the person wore gloves, or if he cleaned it before throwing it into the lake. It's possible the water washed away the prints. It was storming that night, and most of her blood washed off the deck. Blake used luminol and the deck proved to be the murder scene. We know that the DNA evidence under her fingernails belongs to an unidentified male and matches the sample from the envelope."

"So, if we find the person with the right DNA, we have found the one who shot Julie Cromwell."

"Not necessarily," Larkin said. "If we find the person who matches the sample, we can prove he sealed the letter and he struggled with her in the car. What I'm wondering is, if the perpetrator had a gun, why didn't he shoot her inside of the car? She tore him up. Why would he wait until they were outside to shoot her?"

"Maybe she fought him off and was able to get away. He was afraid she would tell on him, so he went after her. He shot her, picked up the money and got the hell out of there."

"That's what the officer on the scene seemed to think."

"But you're not convinced?"

"I can't see someone taking time to wipe his fingerprints off the car, and maybe letting her get away, then going calmly about putting a bullet through her heart."

"Maybe he wiped the car down after he killed her."

"He could have, I guess."

"What did David think?" Ted asked.

"You know David. He said he would make no guesses until he had gone over all the evidence again. He doesn't care how we think it happened. He always says 'People can be wrong, the evidence isn't.'"

"We know that Julie planned her own kidnapping."

"Do we?" Larkin questioned. "Everyone in the family knows she is capable of hatching a scheme like this. Let's say that Tina and her boyfriend knew about the plan, and they decided to double cross Mom for the money. Snake fixes the note and gives it to Tina. Tina plants the note while her mother is out. The boyfriend snatches Mrs. Cromwell, she fights back and he winds up killing her. Tina never planned on it going that far, and now of course she is involved in a murder, so she can't tell."

"Do you think that's the way it happened?"

"Not really," Karl confessed. "We can sit here and make up a scenario for everyone involved, and they would all be possible. What we need is good solid evidence. We're weeks into the case and we haven't eliminated anyone."

"We know that the DNA doesn't match anyone we've tested."

"We can't even say without a doubt, that the person who fixed the note is the one who killed her. I still think we have someone on the inside working with this man."

"There wouldn't have to be a third person involved," Cramer reasoned. "The shooter could have fixed up the note, and Julie brought it home and talked Tina into placing it there, just as she said. Julie could have met the perp, they got into a heated argument, and he killed her."

"Like I say, we could think of a dozen ways it might have happened, but what we need is hard evidence."

"My money's still on the old man," Cramer said. "I think he is tired of her shenanigans, and he knew her history better than anyone. He knew the family would believe she set the whole thing up herself. I think that she finally did something that pushed him over the edge and he hired this mystery guy to whack her..."

"What about the note that Tina said her mother gave her?"

"Maybe her dad persuaded her to lie. Maybe he promised to get her a dress."

"I don't think she would lie for him if she thought he killed her mother."

"So you're saying she would lie for her boyfriend, but not for her dad."

"I'm thinking she wouldn't lie for either, unless she was implicated in the murder. What did you find out from the people who work for Lawrence Cromwell?"

"Everyone said and I quote, 'Lawrence Cromwell is a real nice guy.'"

"What did they say about Mrs. Cromwell?"

"Nobody Liked her."

"Did anyone suggest that he might be having an affair?"

"They didn't even hint at it. To hear them tell it, the guy's a saint," Ted remarked sarcastically.

"What did you think of the Risners?"

"The wife is nuts. The husband seems scared of his own shadow. Do you think one of them might be involved?"

"Well, neither one of them liked her. She might have thought they were helping her and they turned on her instead. They could have gotten their son to fix up and deliver the note."

"What about Cassie Thompson?" Larkin stiffened at the mention of her name.

"The money was an advance against royalties."

"Are you going to tell me a romance writer makes that kind of money? If they do, I'm changing professions."

Larkin laughed. "I made the mistake of saying something like that. I received an enlightenment about the business of love."

"What are you talking about?"

"I mean writing is a lot harder than you think. Look-you may as well know that I went out with her last night."

"Tell me it was because you're investigating her."

"I like her-what can I say?"

Cramer almost said he was a hypocrite, but stopped himself in time. The man had always preached to him not to get involved with a suspect.

"When I interviewed her the other day I found myself asking her out. It's been a long time since I've enjoyed a woman's company so much."

"Did you check to see if her story about the money was true?"

"I thought you did that," Larkin said. "Didn't she give the bank permission to let you view the records?"

"All they let me see was a list of deposits and the amounts. They wouldn't give me any other information unless she signed a paper, or we got a court order."

"I'll give her a quick call and ask her to meet you at the bank to sign the paper. I'm sure it won't be a problem."

Cramer listened as Larkin explained the situation and Cassie sounded irritated as hell, because he didn't trust her. That's what happened when you became involved with a suspect.

"She will meet you at ten o'clock," Larkin said.

"She's not happy, is she?"

"I can't say that she is. Maybe it's for the best."

"You're in love with her." Cramer nodded his head.

"You're crazy," he denied.

"I can't believe it. I am watching the great man fall. I'm thinking black widow here, man. Be careful-okay?"

How Cramer felt about Cassie bothered him. Maybe she had impaired his judgment. He did respect Cramer's opinion.

Larkin looked thoughtful. "I wish I could get Carrie to tell us about her and Julie's past."

"It's really hush-hush," Ted agreed. "These days everyone is open about things like this. I can't imagine them not wanting to talk about it."

"I'm still not convinced there isn't a link between their childhood and the murder."

"It could just be about the money, like you said. That is a million reasons for murder."

"Whoever we're dealing with, they're clever," Larkin said.

"Or just plain lucky."

"The truth is we haven't found a link to any family member, co-worker, or employee of Cromwell's. In questioning the family, we can't tie any of them to a hired killer."

"I'm still thinking it is Cromwell. He hires the killer because he overheard his wife planning this. He goes along letting her work out the details and then he makes a different deal with the accomplice, only he tells the person if they kill her, they can have the whole million. It would be a small price, for getting rid of a big problem," Cramer finished.

"We don't have the evidence," Larkin said.

"The DNA from the envelope is great evidence."

"It isn't worth anything unless we know who contributed it," Larkin reminded.

CHAPTER 10

---◆---

For a station no bigger than Springfield, they had a great CSU team. It had come together by hard work on David Blake's part recruiting people he worked well with.

Barry Talbot, a firearms expert, was self-taught. His interest in weapons had started when he was in Vietnam and carried over into his civilian life. He had a reputation around town and a friend on the police force. His friend involved him in a case and the rest is history. The department began first to use him unofficially, and as he helped them solve more and more cases, hired him as a permanent member of the team.

Larkin, decided to talk with him that day because, not only did he know guns, he also knew people. Maybe he could give them insight about why the killer would use the kind of weapon he had. At this point, he would try anything.

"Thanks for seeing me," Larkin said as he came up to the man studying something under a microscope.

"Always glad to help," he turned and shook hands with Larkin. "What can I do for you, Detective?"

"I know what kind of revolver killed Julie Cromwell..."

"Did you know there is one like it registered to Cassie Thompson?"

"Are you saying it's her gun?" Larkin felt the blood drain from his face.

"The numbers have been filed off, so there is no way of telling for sure. Cramer was curious to see if any of your suspects had permits to carry a concealed weapon. He also asked me to check if anyone owned one fitting the description of the murder weapon. She does, but the catch is, she reported it stolen three years ago."

Larkin let out his breath. It was suspicious, but at least it gave him a little hope that it might not be hers. Maybe someone did steal her gun and used it to kill her step mother, and maybe the moon is made of green cheese, he said to himself.

"I wanted to talk to you before. I told the guys to have you stop by, but they probably forgot."

"I knew you would have something else for me!" Larkin exclaimed.

"Whoa, buddy-I don't know how great it is, but I do have a tip. You need to check out a gun club on the east side of town. The name of it is Shoot to Kill, or something like that. They teach their members to do just that."

"What, shoot to kill?"

"The interesting part is they teach the person to put one bullet directly through the heart and one through the head."

"That is interesting."

"I thought you might think so. They start a newbie out shooting at stationary targets and they graduate to moving ones. They use paper people with a picture of a heart where it belongs, and the point between the eyes is marked by a big circle. You might want to check to see if any of your suspects ever had lessons there."

"I am on it. Thanks, Talbot," he said, slapping the man's shoulder.

Larkin was impressed. Not only was the man good with firearms, he knew what was going on around town. Everyone had talked about the shooter being an excellent shot, and now he had a hot lead to check out about a place that taught their members the two most deadly places to shoot their victims. It had to be more than a coincidence.

The gun club turned out to be a gigantic shooting range in the middle of a forty-acre woodland. It was a huge pit dug out, leaving walls of earth on three sides to make the shooting area safe. One side was for beginners and the other for advanced. They separated the shooters into cubicles and supplied them with earplugs to protect their hearing.

Red flags went up when the owner introduced himself as Mike Risner.

"Are you related to James Risner, by any chance?" Larkin asked as they shook hands.

"If you mean the contractor here in town, the answer is yes. He's my first cousin."

Larkin and Cramer looked at each other. This was very interesting indeed.

"In fact, James and I used to own this place together."

"You don't say?" The two detectives flashed each other knowing looks once more.

"You bought it together then."

"Actually it was our grandfather's place. When he died, we inherited it. What is this about anyway?" Risner had seen the knowing looks passed between them, and frankly cops made him nervous. Organizations who hated guns attempted to shut him down, and cops were always hanging around criticizing him for the way he taught people to shoot. The owner believed in kill or be killed, and a person had better be more deadly than the next.

"Look, all my papers are in order, we keep everything strictly legal."

"Don't get your panties in a bunch," Ted broke in. "We're here about murder."

"Could we close this door?" Larkin asked, rising and already pushing it to. The gunfire was deafening and as he suspected the office was soundproof. Larkin wondered if the man left the door open because he got off on hearing the noise.

"So, what murder are you here to accuse me of causing?" he asked sarcastically.

"We're investigating the murder of James' sister-in-law, Julie Cromwell."

"I heard about that. Do you know who did it yet?"

"Frankly we were hoping you could help us to find the person responsible."

"And pray tell how would I be able to do that?" he said with a smirk on his face.

"She was shot twice; once between the eyes and once in the heart."

"And let me get this straight. Just because this is the way I train people to shoot, you think I'm responsible."

"We didn't say that, Mike." Ted rose from his seat to show that his over-six-foot frame could be just as intimidating. "But we think you may have trained the shooter."

"Look, Detective, we have a membership of over a thousand right now. That doesn't include the people who have dropped out over the years."

"Wow!" Ted exclaimed. He began to pace back and forth thinking about it. What had started out a promising lead was quickly becoming like looking for a needle in a haystack.

"Is your cousin James a member?" Larkin asked.

"Yes-him and all of his family. James is a gun collector, and an excellent shot. Our grandfather taught us to shoot almost before we could walk. His dream was to open a place like this, and James and I caught his enthusiasm. Things never worked out for him, but I was determined to follow through."

"You said that his whole family are members. Are they as good as James?"

"His wife, Carrie, can put out a gnat's eye at fifty paces. Toby is almost as good."

Ted and Karl flashed glances at one another once more.

"You're not accusing one of them of killing Julie Cromwell, are you?" He pushed back his seat as if he was ready to show them the door.

"We're not accusing anyone," Ted said, "but we're checking everyone out."

"Would you mind if we looked over your records for the last five years?" Larkin asked.

"I don't suppose it would do any good to mind," he said, rising. "I will make you a printout." He went to the PC, typed in the information and the printer started spitting out pages.

"Do you know any of the Cromwells?"

"I know Lawrence. He was a member at one time. He tried to teach his wife to shoot, but she wasn't interested. That woman was something else. I never trusted anyone who didn't like guns."

"She wasn't a member then?"

"Oh no. She was too good for the likes of us."

"But she was allowed to come here?"

"A member is allowed to bring any guest as long as they pay for their targets and ammo."

"So a member can bring twenty different guests if they want?"

"There are certain restrictions. They can only bring one at a time and if the same person comes more than three times, he must join or he isn't allowed back."

"I see," Larkin said. "Did Mr. Cromwell bring anyone other than his wife?"

"He brought his kids."

"How many of the children did he bring?"

"He brought all of them. There was a boy and a young girl, with crazy hair and earrings all over. He also brought his oldest daughter. Now there's one that makes heads turn," he said, raising his eyebrows.

Larkin bristled at his description of Cassie, and Ted cast him a warning look.

"How well did the children handle a gun?" Larkin asked.

"All of them did pretty well. The youngest two only came a few times."

"What about Cassie Thompson?" Ted asked.

"She is still a paying member. She hasn't been lately, but she used to come all the time, especially when her dad first joined."

"Mr. Cromwell isn't a member anymore? Why do you think he quit?"

"His wife put up such a fuss about him coming that I guess it just wasn't worth the hassle. That's the idea I got from his daughter. She said the woman couldn't stand her dad doing anything he enjoyed. I got the feeling there was bad blood between them."

Larkin had a gnawing feeling in his gut. He was hoping for new information, but he didn't like hearing this. Cassie hated her stepmother and she was a member of the Shoot to Kill gun club.

"Would you say Mrs. Thompson is a decent shot?" Ted looked at Larkin instead of Risner as he spoke.

"No, her dad was a good shot. His daughter was a crack shot. I often find that women are better than men."

Ted rolled his eyes toward Larkin. There was that warning again.

"Do you sell guns at the club?" Larkin asked abruptly.

"Yes, I do." Mike bristled. "I follow all the rules. No felons, I make them do the waiting period. Too bad, the criminals don't have to follow the same rules. It's the law-abiding citizens that you guys make it hard on."

Larkin and Cramer had heard the same gripes a thousand times.

"Do you have a concealed weapon permit, Mr. Risner?"

"I was the first one in line the day the law went into effect, Mr. Larkin. I'd say that about ninety-nine percent of my membership has one."

"That's a comforting thought," Cramer quipped.

"I know you think the killer is someone I've trained..."

"The possibility is very likely," Larkin agreed.

"What you're not considering is, of the people I have trained, how many have taught their friends and family."

"The thought did cross my mind," Larkin admitted.

He watched Cramer wilt as Mike continued, "Who knows how many people out there shoot to kill? I'm surprised that Springfield Police Department doesn't send their people here to be trained."

"You said that you and James once owned this place together. What happened to that?"

"James was interested in guns, but I was an enthusiast. He liked to build things. Guns were more of a hobby for him. I bought him out about ten years ago and he used the money to go into the construction business. I hear he's quite good. He got himself a deal for a big mall or something?"

"You mentioned he had a gun collection. Did he get any of those guns from you?"

"A few of them." He eyed Larkin carefully. "Why?"

"I was just wondering," Larkin said. "The ones he didn't obtain from you, do you have any ideas where they come from?"

"I think you need to ask James that question, bro," he said.

"I probably will." The look on Larkin's face said he didn't fancy being thought of as the man's bro.

"Tell me, if one wanted to hire a shooter could it be done through the clientele of Shoot to Kill?"

Mike gave a belly laugh. "My clients are all law-abiding citizens, Mr. Larkin. Most of them are rich and powerful people."

Larkin rose from his seat. "We'll be in touch, Mr. Risner."

"Give my regards to Cousin James."

Cramer would have given anything to wipe the smirk off the man's face, but meekly followed Larkin to the door.

"I can't believe you asked him that," Cramer said as soon as they were out of earshot.

"I don't like the man," Larkin informed him. "I think he's one step away from white supremacy, and a step toward the KKK. Of all the people training do you see one black person?"

Cramer looked around. He didn't. "You're not a trusting soul, are you, Larkin?"

"I guess not."

"You should apply that toward your girlfriend," he advised. "She's a crack shot, ain't that what the man said? There was bad blood between her and her stepmother. Is any of this getting through?"

Larkin didn't answer, but he was thinking.

"Don't look so sick," Cramer said after a time. "It sounds like half of the vicinity has been a member here. It doesn't narrow the suspect list down any, does it?"

Larkin didn't tell Cramer that the others hadn't confessed to being glad Julie Cromwell was dead. He had to admit it to himself. Cassie Thompson was rapidly becoming a prime suspect. He made a mental note to check records tomorrow to see how many other guns were registered in her name.

"I skimmed through some of the list while we were sitting there," Cramer said. "Max Daily is on it."

"What do you want to bet that both security people are there? In fact, I bet their company sends all of their people there for training.

"The names were in alphabetical order and I noticed him near the top," Cramer said. "I'll go through the list carefully after we get back and compile a list of the people we know."

"It looks like the list keeps getting longer."

Larkin had never concealed information from his partner before, and the guilt was almost unbearable. He planned to do some investigating on his own first, but he had to level with Ted soon.

CHAPTER 11

———— ◆ ————

Early the next day an officer knocked on Larkin's office door and stuck his head inside. "There is a young man here who says you want to see him."

"What's his name?" Larkin had hopes that Snake or Kyle might be here to confess.

"His name is Toby Risner."

Cramer and Larkin looked at each other completely in shock. They had just been discussing getting a court order to lift the kid's DNA. Every time they called the house, his mother put them off saying he wasn't home. The last time he was camping with friends.

The feeling hit Larkin as the officer showed the boy in. He had seen a picture of him somewhere. Why couldn't he remember where? The kid was a star athlete, on the basketball team. Maybe his picture had been in the paper or on the news. There it was again; that niggling little feeling there was something he knew, but just couldn't grasp.

The kid was big, blond and good-looking. He was polite, and that was hard to find in a boy so young.

"I understand that you want to see me," he said as he took the seat Cramer had just vacated.

"Yes, I do," Larkin finally was able to speak. It was such a shock having him here after trying to get his sample for two weeks. "Are your parents out front?" Larkin was looking through the office doors trying to see who had brought him.

"They're not out there," Toby said. "I came down on my own. I heard Mom and Dad arguing about the DNA test. My father wanted to bring me, but my mother didn't."

"Why do you think your mother was against it?"

Toby shrugged his shoulders. "I'm an only child; my mother is protective."

Larkin nodded his head. "You say your parents don't know you're here?"

"Not really." He looked uncomfortable when Larkin mentioned his parents. "I heard them talking about it and I thought, 'What's the big deal? if just drop by before classes and give my sample.' We're having exams this month and I had two back-to-back study halls," he explained.

"How old are you, Toby?" Larkin asked.

"I just turned eighteen the first of this month. Why?"

"No reason." Larkin knew there could be a problem if they interviewed someone underage without their parents' consent. If they listed DNA from him, some lawyer would step in and deem the evidence inadmissible.

A knowing look passed between Cramer and Larkin. If the kid was eighteen, there was nothing his mother could do about it.

"We'll send you down to David Blake's office in a few minutes, Toby. If you wouldn't mind, I'd like to ask you a few questions first."

"Sure, go ahead," he said casually.

"How did you get along with your Aunt Julie?"

"I can't say that we were close, but I had nothing against her. She was always nice to me."

That was the first time Larkin had heard anyone say something that nice about Julie. Toby didn't say he liked her, but he did not say he disliked her either.

"We know you visited the Cromwell estate on Saturday before Mr. Cromwell found the ransom note. Can you tell us why you went there?"

"It was my birthday, and to celebrate my being accepted at Yale, my mother and dad bought me a new Jaguar. I went over to see if Todd and Tina wanted to go for a ride. They had just gotten up and didn't want to go, so I went to another friend's house."

Cramer was busy writing, only looking up from his notes now and then as Larkin asked the questions. Toby's answers flowed easily. Either be was telling the truth and didn't have to think about his answers, or he had time to rehearse them before the talked to the police.

"Only one more thing," Larkin said. "I hear you're a pretty good shot."

"I guess you could say that." He frowned.

"Have you ever been shooting at the Shoot to Kill gun club?"

Toby frowned. "I've gone shooting there since I was about nine. My dad's cousin owns the place, you know. Why do you ask?"

"Who do you go with?"

"I've gone with my parents. Sometimes I go with Uncle Lawrence."

The boy was intelligent, and he was beginning to become wary of this type of questioning.

"Do you know how your aunt was killed?"

"She was shot... That's what I heard..."

"Do you know where she was shot?"

He stopped. It was dawning on him that he and his family might be suspects.

"No." He looked around as if hunting an escape route. Larkin could see he was uncomfortable. "All I know is what I've heard my parents discussing."

"She had a bullet through her heart and one through her head. Right between her eyes," Larkin said for emphasis.

Toby swallowed hard as if he might be sick. "You don't think it was one of us, do you?" he asked at last.

"Everyone is a suspect at this point, son. Do you know anyone who would want to hurt your aunt or your uncle?"

"No, I really don't."

"I think we're finished except for taking your sample," Larkin told him. "I'll have David do that now."

As Toby followed David out of the room, Larkin called to him, "Thanks for coming in, son. You did the right thing."

The boy stopped and turned around. "Sure-no problem," he said, but he looked troubled as he left the room.

"That was a shock," Ted said after he was gone.

"Yes, it was."

"Think we'll catch a break?"

"I'm really doubtful. If the kid was into this, I don't think he'd be down here. He's intelligent enough to know about DNA and how it works."

"Maybe he doesn't know that we have the killer's DNA."

"It's been all over the news. I'm sure he knows, and even if he doesn't, he has heard his parents discussing it."

"And again I remind you that we don't know if we have the killer's sample. All we can prove is the guy licked the envelope and attacked Mrs. Cromwell in her car."

"I think it's enough to hang the son of a bitch, if we can find him."

"There have been people convicted on less," Larkin supposed, but he wanted to catch the right person, no matter if he was the mysterious donor or not.

"Mama is going to be furious when she finds out her golden boy came down on his own," Cramer said, amused.

"I'd hate to be in his shoes, or James' either when she finds out," Larkin said.

Days later, David Blake was back in Larkin's office.

"Tell me it's good news," Larkin said.

"It is for Snake and Kyle, is that the other one's name? Neither of them matches your sample-and Max Daily isn't your man either."

"Damn!" Cramer pounded his fist on the desk. "I was sure it would be one of them."

"Did you take Toby's sample?" Larkin asked.

"Yes, but it will probably be a few days before I get to it. The big city of London thinks they have a serial killer loose. Someone killed two teen girls. I'm working on the case for the sheriff over there."

"I doubt there is any hurry," Larkin commented. "I have a feeling he wouldn't have volunteered a sample if he was the one."

Cramer doubted it also and could see the lead, which started out promising, heading for the pooper. They still had a bunch of suspects and no evidence against any of them.

"I think I will talk to Larry Cromwell about offering a reward. It might entice someone to come forward with information."

"That's a great idea!" Cramer exclaimed. "I don't know why you never thought of it before."

"Oh-I thought about it, but when you do that, you have to be ready for all the crazies to come out. Every nut in town will be calling with reports about aliens, to it being a mafia hit."

"What else can we do?" There was notable disappointment in Ted's voice. "We have tried to trace the money, and that didn't work. It looks like half of the city trained to shoot at the same place. We can't tie anyone to a hired gun..."

"There is one place we haven't gone, and that is back in time." Larkin sighed.

"That's great. And who do we know that has a time machine?" Cramer asked.

"You watch too many movies." Larkin bent forward and patted the younger man's shoulder. "We'll start with this year and work our way backward. I want to know what was happening in the Cromwells' life from this minute in time, back until the day they were born. The answer is there somewhere; we just have to find it."

"I did make a list of the family, friends, and employees who have belonged to Shoot to Kill, if you think it will do us any good," Cramer said dejectedly.

"Oh, I believe that it was someone who trained there, and I believe our killer is someone on your short list."

"We have Larry Cromwell, Carrie and James Risner, Toby, the two security guards, and Cassie Thompson, but it really doesn't prove anything. Like we talked about, half the population of this city has trained there. A good lawyer would have a field day with us trying to prove we know the killer just because they learned to shoot there."

"We are not going to use it alone. It will be just another piece of evidence against the right person," Larkin said. "You forgot Todd and Tina. Larry taught them to shoot also."

"Larry?" Ted raised his eyebrows.

"He asked me to call him that." Larkin hated making the mistake. Ted already thought him to be too involved with the family.

"They're rich people, Larkin. They know how to sucker people in and use them to their advantage. You've never let anyone do that to you before, and I think it's because of that woman. She has you blinded."

"Don't worry," Larkin said. "I told her I would call her, but I'm not going to. You're right. I'm in over my head, and I need to focus on the case. She's angry at me anyway, so I guess it's the end from the beginning."

"You don't need someone who gets mad because you're doing your job."

"You're right, Ted, I don't."

Just then, the phone rang and Ted picked up. He listened for a few seconds then snapped, "Get a life, lady," and hung up.

"What was that about?" Larkin asked.

"Those dispatch bums must be having a slow day." Larkin could see the people who worked out front laughing and pointing toward his office.

"This woman says she had a for sale sign on her boat, and someone stole it."

"If someone stole her boat she needs to be transferred to burglary."

"You don't understand, Larkin. They didn't steal the boat, they stole the sign."

"You're kidding?" Larkin laughed then. It was just what he needed to relieve some of the tension.

Cramer was now beginning to see the humor in it, and he laughed as well. Thanks to the people out front, the tension was relieved, and thanks to Toby Risner, they had his DNA.

Days later, David Blake came back to Larkin's office with a grin so wide it looked like he had slept with a coat hanger in his mouth. Larkin knew that he had something.

"Man, this job is interesting," he said.

"You've done Toby Risner's DNA, and you have something." Larkin was pleased.

"Is he the one?" Ted snapped impatiently.

"He's not the supplier of the DNA from your envelope, but he is a member of the Cromwell family."

"We know. He's Lawrence Cromwell's nephew."

"Oh, he's much closer than that, I'm afraid."

"How much closer?"

"The boy is Cromwell's biological son."

"Are you sure?" Cramer exclaimed.

"I'm 99.9 percent sure," David said.

Now Larkin could explain the feeling he had every time he saw the boy. At the house, he had noticed a photograph of Lawrence Cromwell when he was about Toby's age, and they were identical. Now it made sense. He didn't know why he hadn't put it together before. It had to be because he had allowed Cassie Thompson to distract him.

"This case gets wilder and wilder," Cramer said after David was gone. "Now what do we do?"

"I'm going to call Carrie Risner at work. We need to have a little talk."

When Carrie came on the line, Larkin told her that Toby had given a DNA sample, and there was dead silence. Larkin said he needed to talk to her and did she want him to come to her house or could she come by the office. She said that she would be at his office in less than thirty minutes.

Larkin and Cramer high-fived each other as Larkin hung up the phone. She was going to be on their territory this time. Larkin told the people working out front to show Carrie in as soon as she arrived.

CHAPTER 12

———— ◆ ————

Visually shaken, Carrie took a seat beside the desk. Cramer found his pen and pad as Larkin began the interview.

"I told you we took your son's sample when we talked on the phone..."

"I know what you found," she said, taking a hanky out of her purse and nervously twisting it, then wiped the perspiration from her face.

"And what was that, do you think?"

"Let's not play games, Detective. You know that Toby belongs to Larry Cromwell."

"Yes, we do. Would you care to explain?"

"You have to understand, Detective. Larry belonged to me first."

Larkin thought it an odd choice of words. "Larry belonged to you?"

"We went together first, but after he met my sister, it was all over for us. She took him away from me as she did everything else. She was younger and prettier, and he fell head over heels."

"I bet you hated her for that," Larkin said.

"At first maybe, but I was accustomed to her taking things from me. They were married soon after they met. Larry moved Julie away from North Carolina and he helped me get away also. I will always be grateful to them both for that."

"Is that when you moved to Springfield?"

"Yes. Larry had saved enough to open a small practice, and a friend of his from school talked him into coming here."

"Who was this friend?"

"It's the district attorney, Deets," she said as if Larkin should have known.

"I moved in with Larry and Julie at first, but I soon got a job at Health and Human Services, and I got my own place. Soon after, I met James and married him."

"What about Cromwell and you?"

"I'm getting to that. About a year after Todd was born, Julie started having an affair. Larry needed someone to confide in and I was there for him. Our affair was brief and by the time I found out that I was pregnant, Julie and Larry had reconciled. I really didn't know who the father was until after the baby was born," she said, hanging her head.

"Have you had him tested before?"

"No, but look at him. A blind person can tell."

"Do you think your husband knows?'

"Men are all blind," she said bitterly. "Neither Larry nor James has ever guessed."

"Did you tell anyone about this?" He was beginning to feel sympathy toward a woman, who clearly hadn't had an easy life.

"No, I didn't. James was ecstatic about the baby. I just couldn't tell him. I didn't want to put a strain on Larry's marriage, when it was shaky at best. I'm not proud of what I did, Detective, but I'm not sorry I have my son. I'm begging you; please don't say anything to anyone about this. If you do, it will destroy my family. Larry might try to take Toby away from me. My husband might leave me, and take Toby. I couldn't stand that, Mr. Larkin. It would kill me. My child means everything to me." Her eyes pleaded with Larkin to understand.

Larkin seemed to consider things for a minute and then he spoke, "I can sympathize with you, Mrs. Risner, but I can't make you any promises. I won't bring it to anyone's attention unless it is necessary to solving this case."

"I thank you, Detective Larkin, and I appreciate you being discreet."

"I appreciate you coming down and straightening this matter out."

"I can go now?"

"One more thing. Did Julie know about Toby?"

She had started to leave, but stopped dead in her tracks. "Oh, heavens no." She smiled as though she had heard a funny joke. "She would have used something like that to control my life, Detective. You don't know her. She was an evil woman."

"Thanks again for coming in, Mrs. Risner," he called after her.

"What I have told you-again I ask you to keep it from Larry and my husband." She looked worried.

"At this point I see no need to tell them," Larkin assured her. "If the secret comes out, it will be you who tells."

"Thanks, Detective. I will be eternally grateful for this."

"Whew!" Cramer exclaimed after she was gone. "No wonder she didn't want us taking a sample of Toby's DNA."

"Can you imagine living with that fear all those years? Thinking any minute someone is going to guess the boy belongs to Cromwell," Larkin said.

"It looks like this murder is bringing out the skeletons in a lot of closets," Cramer said.

Larkin nodded his head. Something Carrie said bothered him. She said if Julie had known about the boy, she would have used the knowledge to control her life.

"I wonder if Julie found out about Toby and began blackmailing her. It would give her a reason to kill."

"She also might hate Julie for taking Cromwell from her," Cramer said.

Larkin had spent the day investigating suspects who owned revolvers and had permits to carry concealed weapons. Everyone on the list from Shoot to Kill did. It was frustrating not to be able to eliminate one person. Cramer had put in his day going over Cromwell's telephone records, looking for suspicious calls made around the time of the murder. There were no calls to anyone other than family members. There were several calls from the residence to Cromwell's office, probably from Mrs. Cromwell, or one of the children. There were a couple of calls to the Risners' residence, but they were family, and even though they didn't socialize, Cromwell had called them when his wife disappeared. Cramer had given up after going back six months, deciding that if someone had called an outsider to help with the kidnapping, that person had not telephoned from the residence. He had also traced the cell phone records. He found out that Larry hardly used his, but Mrs. Cromwell stayed on her constantly. Cromwell's secretary told Cramer, Julie was checking up on her husband.

Larkin had just gotten home when the phone shrilled. "Hello." He was holding the phone with his chin and the side of his face, and trying to feed Ho Bo at the same time, while the dog did excited circles around his feet.

"Karl?" Her voice sent chills through his body. He couldn't help it, it just happened.

"Cassie?" He wondered how she had gotten his home number.

"I thought you were going to call me," she said.

"I've been busy with the case." After a pause, he said, "You sound upset."

"I just turned on the TV and heard my dad offering a half million dollars to anyone with information... "

"I'm afraid I asked him to do that. We simply have no leads."

"Damn! The woman is dead and she's still costing him money."

"She has a right to justice," Larkin said sharply. "Cassie, I think we need to talk..."

She asked him to come for dinner. It wasn't a good idea, but they did need to get some things straight. On his way to her place, he decided to tell her it was best if they didn't see each other for a while. He felt good about his decision until he pulled in front of her building. Knowing he was this close to her made his stomach start to bounce and heave. He was anxious to see her and yet he knew he shouldn't be here.

The aroma from the kitchen greeted him at the door. He was instantly hungry, and when he saw her, it was for more than food.

She pulled back her hair, leaving two ringlets on each side to frame her face. Her silky green dress molded to her form and brought out the color of her eyes. Every instinct told him to run, but his body wanted to stay.

"Hang your jacket in the closet, and join me in the kitchen, will you?" she said as she tossed the salad.

The table was set with candles and flowers and the dress she wore said it wasn't a casual dinner.

"It smells great." Larkin joined her at the bar, sitting close to where she was working. "Can I do anything to help?" What could it hurt having one last home-cooked meal with her?

"I try to keep men out of my kitchen."

"You'll get no fight from me," he said holding up his hands.

"Cassie, I'm sorry about not calling... " The words spilled out after her eyes, softened by the candlelight, questioned him for a time.

"Why do I feel like there's a 'but' here that's bigger than mine?" She gave him a half-hearted smile and sat down across from him at the bar.

"Look, I hope I can just be honest with you," he said swallowing.

"I told you I like honesty the first time we met."

"I've found that people who say that mean they prefer honesty as long as it doesn't apply to them."

"I'm not like most people."

That was certainly true. Larkin had never met anyone like her, and anytime he was around her he was in danger of losing control.

"I'm just going to give it to you straight, then... The first thing they teach you at the academy is, don't get involved with a suspect."

"And, I'm a suspect?" She poured a glass of wine and handed it to him.

Maybe the alcohol would help him relax. He took a sip. It was good wine. He wasn't an expert, but he knew good stuff when he tasted it.

"I found out you're a crack shot, and you're a star pupil at the Shoot to Kill Gun Club."

"So are half of the people around this area," she said impatiently.

"No one else has confessed to hating Julie, and being glad she's dead." His eyes held hers.

"Only because I speak my mind, Karl. Everyone who knew her, hated her-and if the others were honest, they would tell you the same thing."

"You reported a revolver stolen from your place, several years ago."

"That's right. So-you have been investigating me?"

He ignored her question. "It was a .38 caliber..."

"Smith and Wesson," she finished for him. I know where this is heading. The gun is registered to me, and I conveniently reported it stolen. Now you're wondering if I lied."

"Why would you think that?"

"Why else would you be questioning me about the damn gun?" She was irritated and it showed. "It was stolen three years ago. I haven't seen it since. Are you trying to say it's the weapon used to kill Julie?"

"Someone filed the serial numbers off, but from the way your dad described it, it could be. I asked him to come down to the station tomorrow to see if he can identify it."

"Why didn't you just ask me?"

"That would look good in court, wouldn't it? 'Mr. Larkin, how did you determine the gun Mrs. Thompson owned was not the murder weapon?' 'Because she said it wasn't, your honor.'"

"What time is my dad going to the station?"

"Two o'clock."

"I will be there also," she informed him.

He could stop her if he wanted to, of course, but it might not be such, a bad idea. He already knew her dad would never admit the gun belonged to her, and neither would she. He just wanted to see their reactions when he brought it out.

"Are you saying that someone stole the gun to use as a murder weapon?"

"That's one way it could have happened. Another is: you might have reported it missing years ago, knowing that one day you would use it to kill Julie."

Cassie winced. "I thought detectives were supposed to be good judges of character." Her eyes flashed angrily.

"I'm also good at math. Your act in this play adds up to motive and opportunity. You hated her because of the way she treated your dad, and you figured she would be at the drop site watching to see if things went as planned. You could have followed your dad and watched him leave the money, then confronted the woman who had ruined his life.

It could have gotten out of hand and you wound up shooting her. Another scenario would be that you and he acted together."

"My God, you're serious. You think it was one or both of us. If you were good at reading people, Detective, you would never believe Dad   could kill a fly. You would also know that I would never do anything to hurt him. I knew, as worthless as that woman was, he loved her. The way he is suffering now - I couldn't live with myself knowing I put him through this."

Larkin wanted to believe her, but he forced himself to remain hard. There was evidence mounting against her and he needed to put his personal feelings aside and let her know where they stood. He was angry with her and with himself, because she was causing him to doubt.

"Maybe I should go," he said after an awkward silence.

"No, don't." She caught hold of his arm as he started to leave. "Just tell me one thing. Did you only ask me out to see if I would incriminate myself?"

"You know that's not the reason."

"What is the reason, Karl? I have to know."

"Because I like you?" He was afraid to meet her gaze-afraid his eyes would reveal more than he wanted to.

"Why do you like me? Tell me the reason?"

"You're beautiful, intelligent, interesting..."

"And a murderer?"

"Stop it, Cassie," he ordered. "You're a smart-ass, opinionated, stubborn female and those are your good qualities. I don't know why I like you, I wish I did."

She smiled then, wiping the troubled frown from her face and causing Karl to want to reach for her. "I care about you, Cassie, but don't think for a minute it will save you if you had any part in Julie's murder.

"I know that, Karl..."

"There's one more thing. The fact remains that I shouldn't be here."

"Are you saying we can't see each other anymore?"

"Not until the murderer is caught..."

"That may never happen, Karl. You said yourself that you were running out of leads. That's why you had my dad offer the reward."

"I'm sorry, Cass, but that's the way it has to be. And I still think I should go." He hadn't planned it, but his voice softened.

"You can at least stay for dinner. I've already fixed for you. It will be just two friends eating together. Besides, it's almost ready."

"It smells delicious," he said wishfully, suddenly realizing how long it had been since he had a home-cooked meal.

"Its grilled porterhouse, baked potato and tossed salad, with cheesecake for desert. Nothing fancy."

"Sounds like heaven to me," Larkin said. "How fast can you get it on the table?"

A smile spread over her face and Karl realized how happy his staying had made her. It did something to him. No one had ever acted that happy to be with him. It made it twice as nice having a woman as beautiful as Cassie feel that way.

The food was wonderful, but being able to relax and feel at home was soothing to his very soul. Something about being with her did that to him.

"You're so beautiful." The candlelight caused her face to glow and Larkin found it difficult to take his eyes off her.

"You're not so bad yourself." Her voice was husky and low.

"I have no illusions about my looks," he said at last. "I'm average at the very least."

"You really believe that, don't you, Karl? 1 don't know who caused you to feel that way, but I hate her. You're a hotty, and don't forget it. I stole that phrase from Tina," she laughed. "That's the in word for a hunk these days."

Larkin suddenly felt uncomfortable. Did she really believe what she was saying, or was she playing him? His instincts were on high alert. He knew he needed to be careful, because she could distort his thinking. He wasn't his normal self, or he wouldn't be here.

"I see my hotty doesn't take a compliment well," she said, taking her foot and running it along his leg under the table. He wished he had suggested they have their meal at the bar.

"If I didn't know better, I'd say you were trying to seduce me." He stared at her intently.

"If I were trying to do that, I would do this." She stood, then walking around the table, bent and kissed him full on the mouth.

He pulled her onto his lap, his lips devouring hers, his hands tangling in her hair as he held her face.

"Wow!" She said finally pulling back. "I wanted to know what that would be like."

His heartfelt like exploding, his lips and body tingling. "I'm going to leave now," he said, his voice husky with desire.

"Chicken." She smiled and made a flapping motion with her arms.

"I guess I am," he got past the lump in his throat. "We're playing with fire here, and this is completely out of character for me, Cassie."

"I'm sorry, Karl. I promise that I won't compromise your honor." She got up from his lap and began to clear the table. He began helping her, carrying his table setting to the sink.

She stopped and turned toward him. "I've never met anyone like you."

"You mean dull and uninteresting?"

"I mean someone with morals, a sense of responsibility. Someone with integrity. Things I didn't think existed anymore. I look and listen to you and I find myself wondering if you're for real." Her eyes searched his intently as if looking for a flaw.

"Some people interpret that as dull and uninteresting,"

"Not me, Karl. That is what I meant about you reminding me of my dad."

"I'm afraid I'm not near as perfect as you think."

"Be careful, Karl. You're a good man and you know what they say about nice guys. They always finish last."

"They say the good die young. That's the one that worries me. I just haven't found out who 'they' are."

"Not in Julie's case."

"I wish you wouldn't say things like that," he said, catching hold of her arms and looking as though he wanted to shake her.

"You mean things like whoever killed her did the world a favor, or at least my dad." She stared at him like a defiant child. She opened her mouth to say something else, but he stopped her with a punishing kiss, and then let it soften as she began to respond, molding her body to his. Then they were tearing frantically at each other's clothes, not being able to undress each other fast enough. Scooping her up as if she was weightless, he carried her into her bedroom.

Larkin awoke in a cloud of fragrant brown curls, Cassie's head on his shoulder. He remembered making love to her more than once. His head ached, possibly from all the wine. He wished he could turn back the clock. If he could, he would have never come to her house.

Cassie stretched and yawned contentedly, opening her eyes and smiling at him. *No one had the right to look this good in the morning,* Karl thought.

He started to get out of bed, but she pulled him back. "Hold on, I'll get us some breakfast."

"Oh my God!" he exclaimed. "I'm late for work." He scurried around looking for his scattered clothes.

"Wait. I'll turned on the coffee," she told him.

"There's no time. I have to go." He hopped around on one foot looking for his other shoe.

"I made it last night. All I have to do is turn it on." An amused smile played around her lips as she watched his mad scramble to find his clothes.

At the door, she told him, "Karl, stop looking like you murdered your best friend. You had sex with another consenting adult."

He stared at her. "Don't you understand that I could be fired for this?"

"I'm not the kind of girl to kiss and tell... " She let her voice fade away. It was slowly dawning on her. You aren't going to tell on yourself, are you, Karl?"

He never answered, only turned to go. She caught hold of his arm. "Karl," she said, staring up at him, "don't do something stupid. I would never forgive myself if I caused you to lose your job."

"I'm a big boy, Cassie," he said, "I did this all on my own."

"Don't underestimate me, Karl. I usually get what I want."

"It wasn't your fault. I could have gone anytime I liked."

"Don't kid yourself. I knew exactly what I was doing. I seduced you."

"You act like I'm some naive school kid, Cassie. I knew what I was doing also, so don't blame yourself."

"I'm not sorry it happened, Karl," she said, reaching up and kissing him.

"That's beside the point." She felt him stiffen. "I should never have allowed it to happen. It can't happen again. Do you understand?" He stared at her as if willing her to understand.

"Karl, just remember it's only human to fall off of the pedestal once in a while. Call me," she said as he headed out the door.

If anyone out front noticed his disheveled appearance, or that he hadn't changed clothes, they were too polite to comment. Cramer was a different story. "You look like something the cat dragged in," he said as Larkin slid behind his desk.

"Thanks, and good morning to you too," he said as he began to shuffle self-consciously through the reports on his desk.

"So, where were you this morning, and don't say at home, because I called. And don't say you didn't hear the phone, because I know you can hear a pin drop across the room."

"Are you my nursemaid?" Larkin snapped.

"What the hell is wrong with you? Maybe the question I should ask is where you spent last night." Cramer was giving his appearance the once-over. Larkin knew if anyone would recognize the clothes he was wearing, it would be him. No one was more observant than Cramer.

Larkin stopped shuffling papers and faced him. He owed his partner an explanation and he was tired of hiding things. "I stayed at Cassie Thompson's last night," he admitted.

"You slept with her?" Cramer was already closing the door to their office.

"I know what you're thinking and I don't blame you. If it were anyone else who pulled a stunt like this, I would remove him from the case. Just say the word and I will assign you another partner," he said, hanging his head.

Cramer walked around the desk still looking at him. He had always believed his boss to be infallible. He made him into a hero and it was a blow to find out he was only human. "Who knows about this?" Cramer asked at last.

"You, me and Cassie, I guess."

"Good. Now all we have to worry about is her telling on you." Cramer was sarcastic.

Larkin deserved the attitude, so he let it pass. "She's in a position to cause me real trouble. There's no doubt about that."

"What were you thinking? Never mind," Cramer said. "She had to be special for you to ever take a chance like that."

"To tell you the truth, the job was the last thing on my mind at the time," Larkin gave a little half-hearted smile.

"She could cause you real trouble with Deets," Cramer said unnecessarily, for Larkin knew that all too well.

"I have never compromised a case before in my life," he said. "I don't know what's wrong with me."

"Yes, you do," Cramer said. "You're in love with the woman. I just hope she's worth it."

"I hope so too." He stared directly into Cramer's eyes. "Let's get back to business."

"And what would that be?" Cramer asked.

"You couldn't want to work with someone so stupid. Who do you want as a replacement?"

"Karl, I've been with you for three years. If this woman is guilty, you will give her up. I know you. It might destroy you, but you would send her to prison."

"Are you sure about that?" he asked as he stared at the younger man. At this point, he wasn't sure himself.

"You have a sense of justice. You have what my grandpa would call moral fiber. I refuse to work with another partner."

"I can't trust myself when it comes to her. Can't you see that?" He walked to the window and looked out over the yard.

"You will do fine." Cramer came over and stood beside him, patting him on the shoulder. "I trust you to do the right thing, man."

"You might change your mind when I tell you the rest of it," Larkin said, turning to face him.

"The rest of it?" Cramer repeated, frowning.

"The things I've been keeping from you." He might as well lay it all on the line since he was confessing, Larkin thought.

"What things?"

"Mostly things she's said." Karl spread his hands.

"Like what?"

"Like she hated her stepmother. That she's glad that the woman is dead. That whoever killed her did the world a favor."

Cramer's breath caught. "Wow!"

"Yes, and that's not all. I've been checking on how many guns she owns. About three years ago she reported a .38 Smith & Wesson revolver as stolen."

"Do you think it's our murder weapon?"

"I think it could be," Larkin confessed. "You know that the serial numbers were filed off, but Lawrence Cromwell said that Cassie had the revolver modified. She had a pearl handle put on it."

"I'd say that quite a few people have done that," Cramer said.

"I asked Cromwell if he thought he could identify the gun. He said after all this time he doubted it. I asked him to come down tomorrow   and look at it," Larkin said. "Cassie is coming also." He didn't bother telling Cramer it was her idea.

"I don't see much good it will do," his partner said. "Without serial numbers, there is no way to tie them to the gun."

"l want to see their reaction when I show them the weapon."

"You're always one step ahead, aren't you? But - don't you think the killer is the one who stole her gun?"

"She could have planned the murder for some time, and used the gun being stolen as her alibi."

"It's like you said before, Larkin. We don't have any direct evidence against anyone-remember that, and don't look so downhearted. Is there anything else I need to know?"

"She has a permit to carry a concealed weapon."

"What kind is it?"

"It's a .32 Beretta Cougar automatic."

"This lady means business," Cramer said.

"That's what worries me."

"What does your gut tell you about this?" Cramer asked. "Do you think she's guilty?"

"That's just it. I can't trust my feelings on this one, and frankly, it scares the hell out of me. I still think I should step down."

"I refuse to work with anyone else... " Looking up, Cramer let out his breath. "Oh no."

Larkin looked up also to find the district attorney headed their way. "Of all days to put up with that jerk." Larkin lowered his voice.

"Mr. Deets," Cramer greeted the new arrival.

"How's it going, Larkin?" He ignored Cramer and as usual went straight to the top.

"What can we do for you, Deets?"

"How are we proceeding on the Cromwell case?" He kept eyeing Larkin's appearance, where his shirt gapped open and a button was missing. Larkin resented it when the man used "us," or "we," as if he had some big hand in collecting the evidence.

"We hit a snag, actually," Cramer volunteered.

Deets still ignored Cramer and stared at Larkin. "It seems to me that you're concentrating too much on the family as suspects. I talked to Larry yesterday and he said that you want him and Cassie to come in to identify the murder weapon. He said you seem to think it's the same gun that was stolen from Cassie."

"I'm just following the clues, counselor," Larkin said.

"What about this mysterious DNA which doesn't belong to any of the family? Don't you think you should be concentrating on it?"

"Look, I don't tell you how to do your job, and I'd appreciate you not telling me how to do mine," Larkin bristled.

"I don't need to remind you, Detective, that the Cromwells are very influential people in this community. We just can't go around making accusations without evidence to back it up."

"When I'm ready to make an arrest, I'll have the evidence to convict the guilty party, no matter who that may be, Deets." He stared him directly in the eye. "I don't care if it is Cassie Thompson, or Cromwell himself."

"Cassie and I go away back." Deets puffed out his chest. "We met because our dads both belonged to the country club. We dated a few times when we were younger."

Larkin wondered if Cassie had mentioned their involvement to her dad, and the prosecutor was trying to warn him off.

Cramer's eyes met Larkin's. So far, his boss was keeping the green-eyed monster at bay.

"I'm going to have to look her up one of these days," Deets said, "just for old time's sake."

"If there is nothing else you want, Cramer and I really need to get back to work."

Deets glanced at Cramer for the first time, then back to Larkin. "Just remember who we're dealing with here," he said as a parting shot.

"Damn little weasel," Larkin grumbled after he was gone. "He just told me, in not so many words, to look somewhere else besides the family. Lying, keeping secrets, sleeping with a suspect; this case is going to morally bankrupt me before it's over."

Cramer began to laugh. "You're so intense, Larkin. Lighten up."

"I wished I found it that hilarious," he grumbled.

"All kidding aside, partner," Cramer said, slapping him on the shoulder, "you're the most moral person 1 know, and we're going to crack this case together."

"Thanks, man," Larkin said, shaking his hand. "Your confidence means a lot to me."

CHAPTER 13

———————◆———————

Larkin had already signed the revolver out and had it in his desk awaiting Cromwell and Cassie's arrival. As the two walked into his office, his heart did its familiar lurch.

Cassie wore a tight-fitting suit that molded her perfect little bottom. Larkin had to concentrate hard on the business at hand.

After the formalities, Larkin took the gun from the drawer and laid it on the desk in front of them. He could tell by Larry's face he believed it belonged to Cassie. He frowned. "I really can't be sure. It's been three years."

Cassie's eyes narrowed as she bent forward to inspect it. "Can you take it out of the plastic?"

"I'm not supposed to," Larkin said.

"I got a tiny speck of fingernail polish on the handle, underneath," she pointed.

Larkin turned the gun upside down. The spot was there.

"It's definitely the one I had stolen."

Her dad looked sorry she had admitted it. "Now what?" he asked.

"Who knew you had the revolver, Ms. Thompson?" Larkin deliberately addressed her the way she asked him not to. It was his way of letting her know that she was just another suspect.

"The day after I got it, I brought it to the Fourth of July picnic. It's a family thing we have every year. I wanted to show my dad and James. I had just finished the course at Shoot to Kill and I had it customized with a pearl handle. I was proud of it, and I wanted them to see. James is a collector, you know."

"Did anyone take more than a casual interest in the weapon?"

"I never noticed if they did. My dad and James both held it and said it was a nice weapon."

"Was there any particular reason you bought the gun?"

"Actually, there was someone stalking me at the time. That's why my dad wanted me to learn how to shoot."

"So, you did it to protect yourself?"

"This guy claimed to be a fan. When he read my books, he was convinced I was writing about the two of us."

Larkin's eyes flew to hers. It unnerved him to think of some demented lunatic stalking her.

"He would show up at my book signings, follow me to the grocery store, and watch my house. You know - the average run-of-the-mill psycho stuff." Cassie smiled. She knew what it was doing to him and she was enjoying it. "He would call my house and when I answered he would just hang on the line. It became a real pain. That's when I decided to learn how to shoot."

"Did you remember the guy's name?"

"What was his name – Dad - do you remember?"

"Jack Blain, Jack Bran. Something like that?" Her dad shivered, remembering.

"Was there a police report filed on this guy?"

"I assume so," Cassie said. "I had to finally get a restraining order against him before he would leave me alone."

Cramer was writing furiously. "Do you think he might have broken into your house and stole your gun?"

"It could have been him, I suppose," Casie said. "Before he came along I didn't lock my doors. One day he walked right in and went through my things. He left me a rambling love letter pinned to the refrigerator with a magnet. He talked about some intimate underwear I had in my drawer. He said he knew I bought them for when we got together. Now, can you understand why I wanted a gun?" Her eyes met Larkin's directly. He nodded his head.

"If you filed a complaint, his name will definitely be on file," Cramer said.

"So this guy was the reason you bought the gun?' Larkin was thinking they had another suspect.

"I felt scared. I needed it for protection."

"After you got the restraining order, was he ever in your apartment again?"

"I don't think so. He stopped bothering me after that."

"When did you find out your gun was gone?"

"It was a long time after that. I hadn't been to the club for a while and when I decided to go. I looked for the gun and it wasn't there."

"The report said that someone had broken in... "

"I might have been careless and left the door unlocked," she confessed. "I didn't see anything messed up or broken. I just noticed that my gun was gone and I assumed that there was a break-in."

"Who was at this picnic that you talked about earlier?"

"The whole family. The Fourth of July was one of the few times we got together with the Risners. You surely don't think that someone in the family stole my gun?"

"We have to consider everyone. Someone used your gun to commit a murder. We have to look at the people who knew about it. Who besides family was present?"

"All of the staff was working serving food and drinks. The guards and their families were there, a few of Dad's coworkers."

"Was it the same staff as now?"

"I don't think Blanch was here at that time."

"You have the same security guards?"

"Max Daily was here, the other one came later."

"Did either one of the guards take an interest in the weapon?"

"They both looked at it and commented that it was nice. It was just a passing interest," Cassie assured him.

"The other guard. Where is he now?"

"He was killed in a car crash while he worked for us," Larry said.

"That pretty much gives him an alibi," Cramer quipped, causing Larkin to raise his eyebrows. Not everyone understood Cramer's quirky sense of humor. Cassie was trying to hide a half grin herself. *It figures,* Larkin thought. *If anyone would find humor in it, that little smart ass would.*

"I guess that is about all we need for now," Larkin said rising. "Thanks for coming in, Mr. Cromwell," he said, shaking hands with Larry and nodding to Cassie. "I might be calling you if I need more information about the gun."

"You have my number," Larry said as they started to leave.

"You also have mine." Cassie gave him a stare that made him look away. He would have loved to know what she was thinking. He also wondered how much Cromwell knew of his daughter's and his relationship.

After they were gone, Larkin and Cramer looked at each other. "Are you thinking what I'm thinking?" Cramer asked.

"I'm thinking we might have found our mysterious DNA."

It could be the stalker. He knew the layout of her apartment and he might have decided to go back for another look. He could have found the gun, and you've seen these crazies before. He might have found out that Cassie hated her stepmother and he decided to take care of the problem for her."

"What worries me is that Cassie could have known how delusional he was and talked him into doing it for her. It would be perfect. No one would believe a crazy stalker over her."

"You are a trusting soul," Cramer said.

"She could have given him the gun and told him to wait awhile before he did it. She could have then reported the gun missing and then had him wait for the right opportunity. Maybe she even promised him they would be together afterward."

"Gosh, do you believe she's capable of that? This is the woman you're in love with, Larkin, and you don't trust her any more than that."

"I don't know," Larkin said, shaking his head. "It just seems odd that she hated Julie so much and her gun just happens to be the murder weapon. Right now, she is my prime suspect. I hate it, but I can't ignore it."

"Either way, this might be the break we're looking for," Cramer said. "What do you say you and I go down to records."

CHAPTER 14

---◆---

His name was Jack Mann, and Larkin and Cramer were soon standing in front of his last known address.

It was a quiet, older, residential area. The house looked clean, but weather-beaten, and had an apartment on each side.

Larkin knocked loudly on side 92 A and waited, but was greeted by silence. He knocked louder. The banging disturbed an older lady from the other apartment. She opened the door, squinting at them over her glasses. "What do you want? There ain't nobody home," she stated the obvious.

"I'm Detective Larkin and this is my partner, Ted Cramer. We're looking for Jack Mann."

"That deadbeat hasn't lived here in two years. I have a good renter now. She's at work."

"You own the home then, ma'am?"

"Yes."

"And you say that he hasn't lived here for two years?"

"That's what I said."

"You don't have a forwarding address for him, do you?"

"He gave me one." She acted as if holding the door was a chore and Larkin asked if they could come in.

"You have any identification?" she snapped. They showed her their badges and she waved them inside. The scent of mothballs greeted them as they entered.

"I may have thrown it away. I was just glad to get rid of the bum," she grumbled.

"Sorry about the inconvenience, ma'am," Larkin told her.

She hobbled to the kitchen past a steaming bowl of noodle soup and some crackers on the table. Reaching up she pulled down a recipe box from one of her cabinets. Instead of recipes, it served as a tiny filing cabinet.

"Here it is," she said after her search. "He told me to make sure I sent him his mail. I told him to be sure to send me my back rent. I never got it so I threw his mail in the trash."

Larkin looked at Cramer and shook his head. There was no use getting into it with her about the federal offence.

"Is that all you want? I hope so, because my lunch is getting stone dab cold."

Cramer smiled. "Thanks a lot, ma'am, you have been a real help."

"If you find that loser, tell him that Mrs. Geer wants her money."

"Sure thing," Larkin called as they headed out the door.

Jack Mann answered the door rubbing his eyes as if they had awakened him. He was tall, skinny and redheaded, the freckles standing out against his white skin.

"I'm Detective Larkin and this is Detective Cramer, and we'd like to talk to you for a minute."

"What about?" He held the door only partially open and didn't seem eager to let them enter.

"You do any good stalking lately, Jack?" Larkin asked as he practically pushed his way into the apartment.

"Looks like you've come down in the world," Cramer said, looking around the dump he lived in.

"Not all of us have a cop's salary," he spat.

"At least we have a job, Jack. Do you have one?"

"I work at McDonalds over on High. What's this all about anyway?"

"Do you remember Cassie Thompson?"

"Sure, she used to be my girlfriend."

Cramer snorted. "When pigs fly."

"She was. She got mad at me and slapped that restraining order on me. Do you guys have a search warrant?" He seemed nervous when Larkin began looking around.

"Relax, Jack. We're not here to search the place, at least not yet," Cramer said.

"We just want to ask you a few questions," Larkin told him.

"What kind of questions?"

"Are you still stalking women?" Cramer asked.

"I don't do that anymore. I was a kid when that happened with Cassie. "She aint still accusing me of that is she? If she says I am, she's lying."

"We want to talk about that other time, Jack. You got into her apartment, didn't you?"

"No."

"We know you were in there, Jack. We have a copy of that juicy love letter you wrote her. It's in your file," Cramer told him.

"All right... All right. I was in there. All I did is leave that letter, nothing else."

"Now, Jack, I don't think you're being truthful here. Mrs. Thompson noticed that you had messed with her things. You also talked about the panties you said she bought especially for you. Did you look to see if she had other love letters? Maybe finger through her delicate under-things, and get a little thrill?" Larkin had the man squirming.

"Okay... I did look around a little. I wanted to see what she was like."

"I can understand that, Jack," Larkin continued. "A man just wants to know more about the girl he loves."

"Yeah. I used to go to all her book signings. She was always extra nice to me. She let me know I was special. She wrote such wonderful things in my books. I knew she was crazy about me. Then I don't know what happened. All at once, she didn't want to see me anymore. She acted like she was scared of me," he said, shaking his head. "I think one of the guys I worked with told her something bad about me. They always made fun of me when I told them how she felt about me. They were all jealous."

Larkin almost felt sorry for him. He could see how someone could become obsessed with her.

"Now, Jack, I understand how that must have hurt."

Jack nodded his head as he remembered.

"You never went back and visited her place later. Look through her things, maybe take something that belonged to her."

"No..." He shook his head.

"You never found a gun. You might have been angry with her, so you took the weapon?"

"I was never in her house after that. I did watch her from far away, but I made sure she never saw me."

"It seems strange to me, Jack, that her gun was stolen right after she got the restraining order on you. I'm sure about the dates because I looked it up," Larkin said.

"I don't know anything about no gun."

"Has Cassie ever gotten in touch with you for any reason?" Cramer asked. "I mean, you and her were an item once. Right?"

Jack hung his head. "No, I used to stay home just praying she would call. She never did. I'm beginning to think she never cared at all."

"Did she ever talk to you about killing someone for her, Jack?"

"No. Why would you say a thing like that?"

"Did she promise if you would kill her stepmother for her that you two could be together?"

"No. She told me if I didn't leave her alone she would shoot me. All I did is told her how much I loved her."

Now Larkin did feel sorry for him. "Did you ever see her gun?"

"What is all this about a gun? I told you, I don't know anything about a gun."

"Have you heard about Julie Cromwell being murdered?" Larkin got down to the practical details.

"Who?"

"Julie Cromwell, the plastic surgeon's wife; the one who was kidnapped and murdered."

Larkin watched as recognition dawned on his face. "Yeah, I saw it on the news."

"Did you know that she was Cassie Thompson's stepmother?"

"No shit! She must be feeling awful. You think I should call and tell her how sorry I am?"

"No, no," Larkin reminded. "You're forgetting the restraining order, Jack."

Larkin flashed a look at Cramer, who had a grin on his face: Nothing like giving a stalker a reason to start chasing his victim again.

"I guess you're right," he said after thinking it over. "Besides, I kind of got another girl now. She's not near as pretty as Cassie is, but she's nice. I think she likes me too," he said, turning a bright red.

Larkin couldn't help but wonder if he was stalking another one, but kept it to himself.

"Let's get back to the gun, Jack. We think the gun from Cassie's apartment was the one used to kill Julie. It was the same weapon that disappeared right after you and she had your problems."

"You think I stole it?"

"We thought it may be possible," Larkin admitted.

"Well, I didn't."

"Okay, Jack," Karl said, patting him on the back. "I believe you, but I don't know if my supervisor will, so that causes a little problem."

"What do you mean?" His eyes shifted from Larkin to Cramer and then back again.

"My boss is going to want proof."

"How am I going to be able to do that?"

"What we need from you is a sample of your DNA. Do you know what that is?"

"I'm not stupid. I watch TV."

"Well, if you wouldn't mind giving us a sample, I'm sure we can clear this right up," Larkin said.

"You don't have to take blood, do you? I have tiny veins, mine is hard to get."

"Actually, Jack, all we have to have is your salvia."

He looked puzzled, so Larkin explained, "We already have the perpetrator's DNA"

Jack smiled, showing stained half-rotten teeth. "What did the guy do, slobber all over his gun?"

"Something like that," Larkin said. He flashed a warning glance toward Cramer, who was dying to laugh.

"How do we do it?"

"I just happen to have the stuff I need right here in my pocket."

In the car, Cramer took a good belly laugh. "You know if he's our guy his lawyer is going to say you tricked him into giving the sample."

"There are two against one. We'll lie through our teeth if we have to."

"This case has corrupted you," Cramer said, looking at him out of the corner of his eye. Never would the Larkin he knew have suggested lying about anything.

"We need a break in the worst way." Larkin grinned.

Back at the station, Larkin took his precious sample straight to David Blake. He also asked David if he had run their mystery guy's DNA through CODIS again. He said he had, but to no avail. David also promised to run Jack Mann's through as soon as possible. Larkin left his office down hearted, but still trying to remain optimistic. They still had Jack Mann's DNA, and he just might be the one.

Larkin and Cramer started their day in a shot-down mood. They were weeks into the case and out of leads. David Blake had just informed them that Jack Mann was not the mysterious donor of the DNA.

"It doesn't mean he wasn't the one who shot her," Cramer said. "That he isn't the one who stole the gun."

"No, it doesn't," Larkin agreed, "but I think he was telling us the truth. He's probably out stalking someone else, but at least he is leaving Cassie alone."

Cramer shook his head. "Cassie Thompson admitted the revolver was hers..."

"And it is the murder weapon. That has to mean something. Either someone at the picnic saw the gun and decided to take it, or later they decided to kill Julie with it. "

"What's the other?"

"Or, Cassie decided to report the gun stolen so she would have an alibi and she planned to kill her stepmother with it at a later date," Larkin said. He had so wanted Jack Mann to be the one implicated in the murder. He wanted anything that would clear Cassie.

"Where do we go from here, partner?" Cramer asked.

"I think we need to go back to the beginning," Larkin said. "I am convinced that Julie was murdered because of some other reason than the money. I suspect it is a family member. That group just has too many secrets, and I think we have only scratched the surface. We have been watching the family's spending habits, and there hasn't been any excessive spending by anyone. I think the thing with the money was just to throw us off track."

"They might just be sitting tight until the heat is off."

"We can't find a family member or an employee who is his financial trouble. Actually, every one of them is pretty well off," Larkin said.

"I never have had a case to stump me like this one."

"You're right. Not one of them seems to be hurting for money," Cramer agreed.

David Blake knocked and entered the office wearing the wide smile that said he had good news. "Want some good news?" he asked.

"We could use some right about now." All of Larkin's senses were on high alert.

"We have your DNA."

"Our mystery guy?" Cramer was off the corner of the desk, and on his feet.

"I thought you said Jack Mann was not our boy?" Larkin dared to hope.

"Oh, it isn't Jack. Our mystery man is some sleaze-ball named Danny Preston. The special victims unit picked him up last night for rape. The woman identified him. When they gave me the DNA I recognized it before we even run the tests."

"You did a thorough check to make sure?" Larkin was afraid of being disappointed yet again.

"It could not be anyone else."

Larkin and Cramer high-fived each other, with a resounding, "Yes."

CHAPTER 15

———————◆———————

The room was small and dim Like Danny Preston's life. A lone light bulb hung from the ceiling causing more shadows then light. That bitch in the uniform had questioned him for hours, and wouldn't allow him a cigarette. Hell-he needed a stiff drink. He was only here because that bitch had led him on and then gone cold on him; he knew she was putting out for anyone in pants. He never let her get away with it he had taken what he wanted. He didn't know what was going on, but a few minutes before there had been a knock at the door and the bitch that had been harassing him sent her male friend to talk to someone. After that, they both did a disappearing act. Now he watched as two males, one dressed in nice slacks and a pullover shirt, the other in a police uniform, converged on where he sat at the end of a long table. Just their presence was intimidating. They were both big guys, well over six feet he judged, and their size overwhelmed the small room. The well-dressed one sat closest to him, the other stood over by the door. Neither of them spoke for some time.

Danny swallowed. The silence was more unnerving than the harassment he had been going through.

"Hi, Danny," the man beside of him finally spoke. "I'm Detective Larkin and this is my partner, Ted Cramer," he indicated the big guy by the door. "We want to talk to you for a little while."

The guy could be as nice to him as pie, Danny thought, but he wasn't telling him shit. "I told that woman already that it was consensual sex. How many more people are they going to send in here to harass me?"

"I think you're confused, Danny," the soft-spoken man said. "This isn't about the rape, this is about Julie Cromwell."

Danny's heart dropped and so did his color. "I don't know anyone by that name. I have no idea what you're talking about."

Cramer had moved closer and taking his fist, he banged the table hard, causing Danny to jump. "Give it up, creep." He bent close to the other man's face. "We have your saliva on the envelope, and your skin under a dead woman's nails."

"I don't know what you're talking about," he snapped.

"Danny, I'd really like to help you," Larkin's voice was smooth, "but you're going to have to talk to us."

"I know the old good cop, bad cop routine," he sniffed. "I've been through it before."

Cramer walked around him back and forth a few times and then he bent toward his left ear. "The trouble is, man, we're both bad cops. We've worked long and hard on this case, waiting for the person with the right DNA, and frankly, we're both getting a little edgy. My friend here might seem pleasant to you," Cramer said, putting his arm around Larkin, "but you haven't pissed him off yet. I've seen him choke a little perp like you until they turn blue. He knows how to take their shirt and tighten it against the old Adam's apple until their eyeballs bulge, and he can do it without ever leaving a mark."

Danny looked around and swallowed again.

"You're going to have to teach me that trick, ol' buddy." Cramer looked from Danny back to Larkin, and walked over to stand once again by the door.

"Danny, you can see my friend here is getting anxious. I can only control him so long."

Danny looked at Cramer, who stood clinching and unclinching his fists, and Larkin could tell he was getting nervous.

"We have your prints on the murder weapon. Hell, you don't have to talk," Cramer said. "Come on, Larkin, let's book him for murder one and get the hell out of here.'"

"That's a lie," Danny blurted.

"What's a lie?" Cramer came back to stand over him

"You don' t have my prints on any gun."

"How do you know the murder weapon was a gun?"

"I listen to the news. I know the broad was shot."

"There was an attempted rape against her also," Larkin spoke up.

"That's your specialty, right, pervert," Cramer gritted close to his face. "You' re so ugly; you can't get a girl, so you have to rape them."

"You're no dream date yourself."

"My ass would make you a Sunday face," Cramer spat.

"Are you going to get him out of here?" Danny blurted.

"I'll make him leave, but you have to talk to me."

Danny thought about it for a minute. It did look bad for him. They could really pin her killing on him. He knew they didn't have his prints, but he had licked the envelope, and he had tried to get some from the little whore, and she did scratch him pretty badly. He had heard that the police found her dead, but he couldn't see any way on earth they could link him to her, until now.

"Let's face it, Danny. We have enough to put you in the electric chair." Larkin moved closer to him. "It would be in your best interest to tell us your side of the story."

Danny licked his lips. He doubted that anyone would believe his story even if he told it. Hell, he wouldn't believe it himself if someone told it to him.

"The way I see it, Danny, you need a friend. The people you're dealing with have money and good lawyers. In fact, the DA is a friend of Lawrence Cromwell's. They're wealthy, you aren't. I know life has been tough for you, Danny, and you need a break. If you tell us what happened, I may be able to help."

"No cop ever helped me," Danny said, but Larkin knew he was breaking him down.

"It looks like you don't have any choice, shithead," Cramer hissed.

"Okay... Okay... I'll give you my story, but you have to get him out of here." He pointed at Cramer.

"Let me just take the little weasel," Cramer said, catching him in the front of his shirt. "Just let me slam him up against the wall a few times. No one will ever be the wiser."

"You go on, Cramer. He's going to talk to me, right, Danny?"

Cramer still held his shirt and glared at him for a few seconds, then gave him a push backward that almost overturned his chair. "You had better sing like a song bird, or I'll be back. I've beat my head against a stone wall for weeks on this thing and someone is going down."

After Cramer was gone, Larkin took out a tape recorder and set it on the table. "You don't mind me taping this do you, Danny?"

"Don't turn that thing on yet. I didn't say I was ready to make a statement."

"It's procedure, Danny. I have to tape it. There is just the two of us now."

"I wanted to talk off record first."

"That would take too much time. I know my partner, and he will be back before long."

Danny's eyes darted toward the door. "Where did you find that psycho, anyway?"

"You haven't seen him at his worst, I'm afraid. They put him with me because I can calm him down sometimes. No one else can."

"Okay, turn the damn thing on, but I'm telling you right now, you aren't going to believe me."

"Why wouldn't I believe you, Danny?"

"'Cause it sounds ridiculous to me, and I'm the one it happened to. I really don't know where to begin?"

"Start with how you became involved in the kidnapping. I'm going to turn this on now."

"I was just sitting there in the dump where I live, thinking about how crazy my life had been, and all of a sudden the telephone rings. On the other end of the line is a weird voice that calls me by name and asks me if I would like to make a half mil. This gets my attention fast."

"You say the voice was distorted. What do you mean?"

"It was like the voice vibrated."

"You didn't recognize it."

"No. When I asked who they were, they said it wasn't important, did I want to make the money or not."

"Was this voice male or female?"

"I couldn't tell."

"I'm Detective Karl Larkin and it is 3:15 PM, May 14, 2005. I am about to interview Danny Preston about the kidnapping and murder of Julie Cromwell. Danny, is the statement you're about to give of your own free will?"

"Yes…"

"Have you been read your Miranda rights?"

"Several times."

"Did you agree to talk to me without the presence of a lawyer?"

"Yes."

"Now, Danny, about this voice. You say you had no idea who this person was, but they called you by name?"

"Yes. It sounded so weird I almost hung up on the bastard, but then it started talking about the money."

"I would say that the person had a distortion device," Larkin said.

"I don't know what was wrong, but it sent chills down my spine."

"You said they offered you a proposition."

"Yes. I asked them who I had to kill for that kind of money and they said that this Julie Cromwell just wanted to see if her husband loved her enough to pay a million dollars to get her back.

"I remember saying that no woman was worth that kind of money … Kind of making a joke out of it, but this thing didn't laugh. The voice said to me 'In or out Danny. I haven't got time to fool with you.'

"I asked what was going to happen to the other half million."

"And what did it say?"

"It said I didn't have to worry about the other, just to make sure I took only my share."

"What did the voice ask you to do?"

"It said to take a piece of white bond paper, and cut out words and letters and paste them on the paper. That way the police couldn't trace my writing. The voice told me to write it down, and put it on the paper just like they said."

"Do you still have the original copy?"

"No. The voice said to throw it away. I was even told to paste Cromwell's name on the envelope."

"I'm surprised the voice didn't tell you about the DNA."

"All I had was envelopes you have to lick, but they did ask me if the police had my sample on file. I said no, because at the time they didn't. The voice also warned him to stay out of trouble and keep a low profile about spending the money."

"You didn't do that, did you, Danny?" He shook his head and Larkin continued, "You said you didn't recognize the voice, but do you have any idea who this person could be, or where they know you from?"

"Not a clue."

"Think, Danny. It has to be someone who knows the Cromwells and you also."

"That's what's so crazy. I never heard of the Cromwells until all this happened. Don't you think I've strained my brain trying to come up with an answer to that question? The voice echoed and rattled so much there was no way of knowing if I had ever talked to this person before."

"Okay, then what did you do?"

"The person assured me that it was all like a big joke and not really a kidnapping at all. It gave me the time and place that Mrs. Cromwell would meet me to pick up the note."

"Where did the voice say to meet her?"

"I was to meet her on restaurant row in McDonald's parking lot. The voice told me what kind of car she would be driving and that she would be sitting in the driver's seat. I had to get in on the passenger side and give her the note. The voice said to wear gloves because of fingerprints. Mrs. Cromwell wore gloves also. She was going to take the note home and make sure she left it where her husband could find it."

"When you went to the restaurant and delivered the note, was there any communication between the two of you?"

"Not really, except..."

"Except what?"

"I had asked the person I talked to on the phone how I was to know I wasn't being double-crossed. The voice said that when I

PLOT TWIST

delivered the letter, Julie would give me a thousand dollars in one-hundreddollar bills... "

"Did she?"

"Yes. When I got there, her car was already on the lot and she was sitting on the driver's side. After I got into the car, I asked her if she had my money. She asked me if I had the note, and I gave it to her. She handed me the envelope with the money. I checked it and it was all there. She said she would see me Monday evening at the drop site. I got out of the car and left."

"Did you go straight home after that?"

"I made only one stop and that was to pay my rent. My landlord was threatening to kick me out. That dump goes for two hundred a month, and I owned two months' rent so I had money left. When I got back to the apartment, the phone was ringing. It was that creepy voice asking me if things went as planned. I said that they had and it began to give me further instructions. I was to go to the waterfront and wait until Lawrence Cromwell delivered the money."

"Where were you told the money would be dropped?"

"He was supposed to put the money in a boat that was tied to the dock."

"What was the name of this boat?"

"I don't remember the name. The voice described it to me, and I used to go down to the docks a lot. I remembered the boat for it looked abandoned. It had been tied up there as long as I can remember, and I never saw anyone take it out."

His story seems to fit so far, Larkin thought. "Did you do anything else at the docks, Danny, except wait for Lawrence to leave the money?"

"Like what?" Danny squirmed in his seat.

"Now, Danny, if I'm going to help you, you're going to have to tell me the whole story."

"I am telling you the whole story"

"We know you had contact with Julie Cromwell. You can't deny it, because your skin and hair was under her nails."

"Okay, I get to the lake early and I see her car parked behind the building. I got to thinking. If she's having problems with her old man, she might be in need of a shoulder to cry on. She might be

132

in the mood for a little playing around. When I delivered the note to her, I couldn't help but notice what a looker she was. I slipped in the passenger side of her car and started to get a little friendly. The woman went ballistic, scratching, biting, and hitting me in the face."

"So you became angry, and you had a gun with you, so you decided to pop her."

"Hold on, cowboy. I hate guns. I don't want them near me. I didn't bring one, because I never owned one."

"What happened next?"

"I thought to myself, I don't need this shit. I'll just wait until the old man delivers the money and I will take my share and get the hell out of there. After I picked up my share of the take, I could get all the women I wanted."

"So, you didn't get the whole million?"

"No, the money was supposed to be in two identical bags, and I was to take one and leave the other. That is what I did."

"What happened to the other bag?"

"I have no idea. I assumed that the person with the crazy voice got it."

"But you don't know who that was?"

"I told you no. I didn't recognize the voice and I never saw the person."

"What did you do after you got out of the car?"

"I hid on the other side of the building until I saw Cromwell pull up and leave the money on the boat. I waited a few minutes to make sure the cops weren't with him, and then I grabbed my money and got the hell out of there."

"You only took one bag of the money?"

"Yes, the voice told me to make sure I left the other."

"When you took your money, did you notice that there was indeed another identical bag?"

"Yes, there were two bags."

If Danny Preston was telling the truth, someone else had taken the other money.

"Where was Mrs. Cromwell while all of this was going on?"

"Hell if I know. She jumped out of the car and went running. She   went one way and I went around where I could watch the deck."

"Where is this money now?"

"It's in a safe place."

"You know you're going to have to give it back, Danny. It's not your money."

"It is my money. I made a deal with the Cromwell woman. I carried out my end, and it's my money." He pouted.

"You extorted money from Lawrence Cromwell. That's a felony."

"It was her money also. I did a job for her, and was paid for it."

Larkin had to think about that one for a second. Some shyster lawyer probably could make a case with that in court.

"Danny ..."

"I spent it."

"You spent five hundred thousand dollars in three weeks? What did you buy?"

"Things."

"What things? What do you have to show for five hundred grand?"

Larkin reached over and flipped the recorder off. "You know, Danny; I'm going to give you a break. I think you might feel more like talking to me after that." He knew that the special victims unit had picked him up and had been interrogating him since early morning, and he had kept asking for a cigarette and something to drink. He hadn't had lunch and neither had Larkin.

"I could use a sandwich and a Coke. I need a smoke also."

"I'll have them bring you an ashtray and your cigarettes. I'll have someone run out and get us some lunch—but, Danny, after that, we're going to have to get down to the nitty-gritty. I need you be truthful with me, all right?"

"I will." The damn cop thought if he tossed him a few crumbs, he would tell him just what he wanted to know. The damn moron thought he could bribe him with a Big Mac and fries.

Larkin left him alone to eat his meal and smoke because he wanted to discuss the interrogation with Cramer. "I know you heard what's going on." The room had been bugged so Cramer heard the conversation from outside.

"Yeah," Cramer said. "It sounds right on about him delivering the note to Julie. It fits with her giving the note to Tina and her putting it where Cromwell would find it. It also lines up with what Cromwell says about the money, but Danny could have taken both bags. What do you think of his story about the crazy voice on the phone? It seems a little far-fetched to me."

It was some time before Larkin commented. "I believe him, it's just crazy enough to be true, but we'll know more after the rest of the interview."

Cramer knew what was coming next. Larkin was the best he had ever seen. He could turn a perp inside out, and God help him if he was lying, because before Larkin was done, you would think he had been administered truth serum. Danny Preston might think he was smart, but he was no match for Larkin. Cramer was looking forward to this, so much so, that he had made it possible for a new recruit to be present as they listened.

Bobby Tate had wanted to be a detective as long as he could remember, but he also knew that the exam was difficult. He was set to take the test anytime and he had confided to Cramer that he was on the verge of backing out. Cramer thought that watching and listening to Larkin interrogate Danny Preston might make him determined again. Cramer would just beat the little perp into the floor. He hated the smug son of a bitch. That is why Larkin did all the intense interviews.

Cramer and Bobby gathered on the outside of the one-way mirror along with two or three other cops. Deets also came to watch Larkin perform. *That's what it was, a performance*, Cramer thought.

Danny looked up as Larkin came into the room and took his same seat.

"Have a good lunch?" Karl asked.

"It wasn't steak, but it hit the spot." Danny felt much better. He hadn't done anything but fulfilled a contract with Julie Cromwell. He would be eating steak every meal when this was over. He could afford a good lawyer now. One who would prove he wasn't involved in a real kidnapping and murder. He was never going to tell them where the money was. He had earned it and no one could make him give it back. The money was his one-way ticket out of the hellhole where he lived. His wife, Dora, wouldn't hear of him coming home, but she was always trying to bleed him dry because of the kid. It was going to fry her when he took the money and went straight to Mexico. It would serve her right. He smiled as he thought about it.

"Are you ready?" Larkin started to turn on the recorder.

"Watch the master," Cramer said, punching Bobby's arm. The other two guys nodded in agreement. They had watched him before.

"Yeah, but I've told you everything."

"I doubt that, Danny." Larkin's voice had changed slightly, causing Danny to look up abruptly.

"Let's get on with it." Danny steeled himself to endure more hours of the same questions.

"I think my question right before lunch was, where is the money?"

"I told you that I spent it."

"And I told you that I didn't believe that."

"It doesn't make a shit whether you do or not, that's my story."

"Okay, Danny. We'll heave it go for now. You said you took the money and left after the attack on Julie Cromwell. "

"I didn't say I attacked her. She attacked me."

"Her sweater was torn, she had bruises and she wound up dead, Danny. I'd say that was an attack."

"I noticed she was good-looking. I made a pass..."

"She rejected you, Danny. Women have been doing that all of your life, haven't they? That's when you decided to kill her. Right?"

"I didn't kill the bitch. I told you that." His voice was shrill.

"And you expect us to believe that."

"I thought you believed me."

Larkin gave a sarcastic laugh. "I know, I know. Some mysterious voice hired you over the phone to feign a kidnapping plot, blah, blah, blah, blah. What do you want me to believe...? That this disembodied voice followed all of you to the lake and shot her?"

"Yes... I guess. I don't know. I don't know who shot her. I only know that it wasn't me."

"How did you get away?"

"My car."

"Your car was at the lake?"

"There's a path through the woods. I parked my car on the other side and when I left the boat, I took the path back to my car."

"How long is the path?"

"Hell, I don't know. I didn't measure it."

"You can judge distance," Larkin gritted.

"I don't know. It's a quarter of a mile maybe."

"You're a little guy, Danny. That amount of money is heavy. You had to struggle with it."

"I stopped a few times... "

"Did you stop long enough to hear anything that was going on at the lake?"

"I heard two shots. That's all I heard. I was almost to the car by that time. When I heard the shots, adrenalin kicked in. I grabbed the bag and ran as fast as I could, hoping my piece-of-shit car would start."

"Where you scared, Danny?"

"Hell yes, I was scared."

"And why was that?"

"I had a gut feeling something had gone wrong. I knew someone had gotten shot, and I didn't want to be next."

"So your car started and you drove off into the sunset with the money thinking you were going to live happy ever after."

"Something like that."

"There's only one thing wrong with that happy little story, Danny."

"What's at?"

"I don't believe a word of it."

"That's the way it went down. I don't care if you believe it or not..."

"This is what I believe, Danny." Larkin bent close to his face. "I think you brought a gun with you on the intent of raping Julie Cromwell. I think she put up a fight and you shot her. Then you took the money and left the scene."

"I told you that I don't own a gun..."

"It wouldn't be hard to pick up one, in your line of work. Someone stole this one from Cassie Thompson's apartment. The only thing we haven't done is connect you to the theft."

"Who the hell is she?" There were beads of sweat forming on his forehead an upper lip.

"I was hoping you could tell me how you know her..."

"I've never heard of anyone named Cassie Thompson before in my life."

"She's related to the Cromwells. Now does it ring a bell? You stole the weapon from her place three years ago. You do any burglaries on the side, Danny?"

Danny almost wished that the young guy was back. Larkin had changed into a relentless predator that was determined to pin everything on him from burglary to murder.

"You're facing some serious charges here."

"I want my lawyer!" Danny balked.

"Who is your lawyer, Danny? We'll let you call."

"I don't have one yet. I was planning to get one though."

"You were going to pay with the ransom money, right?"

"Yes. No...I don't know."

"The trouble with that, Danny, is, you spent all the money. You just pissed it away." Larkin spread his hands.

Danny swallowed. He could call a lawyer, but he didn't know a good one. He had only had the ones appointed by the court: They didn't know their asses from a hole in the ground. He especially didn't know anyone who he could pay with extorted money. It had been a threat to get Larkin to let up on him, but he hadn't taken the bait.

"You want us to assign you a lawyer?"

Danny thought for a second. Those guys were all amateurs that hadn't had a real case before. He knew that he was going to need a good one to get him out of this mess. "I guess not. At least not yet," he said.

"So let's get this straight. You are declining having a lawyer?"

"Yes... Yes. I'm declining," Danny said sarcastically.

"I don' t know if that's a smart idea, Danny. You're facing some serious charges."

"I don't need a lawyer, 'cause I didn't do anything."

"Okay, Danny. It's your call."

"I didn't kill anyone."

"You know it's only a matter of time before we connect you to the gun."

"I'm telling the truth, man. It wasn't me who killed her."

"You're going to have to prove that, Danny. We need evidence. You just can't say you're innocent. We have you at the murder scene; we have your DNA under the dead woman's nails. We have nothing on anyone else. All we have from you is a mysterious voice hiring you for a fake kidnapping. You know what everyone is going to say, don't you, Danny? They're going to say that it was a real kidnapping, and attempted rape that ended with murder. They're going to say that it was you alone, and that it was for a million dollars."

Danny put his head down on the table, rolling it back and forth on his arms. He was in deep shit here and he knew it. He had to think of something quick.

"I know," he said raising his head. "You can give me a lie detector test."

"Don't waste our time, Danny. We can't use that evidence in court."

"It can prove I'm telling the truth, Larkin. You're right. No one will believe I didn't do it on my own. They're going to try to fry me for that broad's murder. You got to help me."

"Why should I do that?" Larkin faltered. "We have enough right now to charge you with her murder."

"Please... Please. I have a wife and little girl."

"Yeah, you're a pillar of the community."

"I'm telling the truth, Larkin." He caught hold of the detective's arm. "If you will give me the test, I will tell you where the money is."

Larkin paused as if to think, and then he said, "I will make a deal with you, Danny. If you give up the money first, I will see to it you have the test."

It was Danny's turn to think for a second. He wanted that money in the worst way. He had it in his possession. All of his dreams were finally within reach, and this was the reality. It would do him no good if he were dead, or had to spend the rest of his life in prison.

"Okay-okay. It's at the bus station in a locker. If you have a pencil and paper, I'll give you the combination."

"Oh, one last thing, Danny. Have you ever been a member of the Shoot to Kill Gun Club?"

Danny laughed. "I told you I hate guns. Do you think I've ever had money to do that? That place is for snooty rich people."

Outside listening Cramer and Bobby high-fived each other. Cramer had never seen anything like it: the way Larkin worked a perp. That was as slick as hair jell, how Larkin had gotten him to give up the loot, and take a polygraph, and the guy thought it was all his idea.

"Way to go." Cramer slapped Larkin on the back as he walked out the door. "We got the bastard now."

"Don't be so sure." Larkin frowned. "What he's telling us is crazy enough to be true."

"You actually believe that someone else killed her?"

"I have always thought that someone got wind of what she was planning. They viewed this as an opportunity to take care of her. I think they used old Danny here for the fall guy."

"Who do you suspect?"

"It is someone close to the Cromwells. I know Danny has a connection to one of them. When I question him again, I'll find out which one. Right now I want you to get over to the bus station and get that money." He handed Cramer a piece of paper with a combination.

"Do you think it's there?"

"That's what we have to find out. In the meantime, I'm going to get in touch with Buddy Farrell."

"Gotcha," Cramer said, pulling Bobby along with him.

Cramer knew that Buddy Farrell was the best around to do the polygraph. His office was in Columbus, but Larkin might just get lucky and find him in his office.

"I'll have my cell phone with me," Cramer said as he and Bobby headed out. "I'll give you a call as soon as we have it."

CHAPTER 16

———— ◆ ————

B uddy Farrell was out, but his secretary told Larkin she would have him call as soon as he returned. That should gave Cramer enough time to find out if the money was indeed in the locker

Buddy called an hour later to set up the appointment for the next morning. It would do Danny good to cool his heels a while, Larkin thought.

Waiting for Buddy's call had kept him in the office past quitting time and he was there to get Cramer's call saying they had the money. It was right where Danny said it would be. It was all there but a thousand dollars, which surprised both detectives.

Buddy Farrell showed up around nine o'clock to give Danny the polygraph. Larkin had worked on a list of questions he gave the man, who only looked at him incredulously and handed the list back to him.

"All I need you to do is brief me on the case. I will ask my own questions."

"I'm not sure..."

"I'm sure," Buddy bristled at the infringement on his territory.

There was one answer that Larkin was dying to know. Did Cassie Thompson hire Danny to kill her stepmother. He had to find out or go crazy. Something inside of him said she would never do such a thing, but he had to be sure.

Cramer had to smile at the clash of wills. Larkin liked things done his way, and it was easy to see Buddy had his own ideas about how to do his job. Farrell finally stuck the list in his pocket, but Cramer suspected that was where it would stay until he had a chance to chuck it in the closest trash can.

Larkin asked if they could be present while he was doing the test, but Farrell told him politely that the perp wouldn't be as nervous if it was just the two of them. Larkin was shot down at every turn, and finally resigned himself to the fact that he would have to trust the man to do what was right.

Cramer briefed him on the case as they knew it and Buddy assured them he would ask the right questions. Danny was taken to the room Larkin had set up for that purpose.

"I don't know why we couldn't be there," Larkin grumbled. Cramer noticed he hadn't even touched the coffee one of the office girls had brought him. That was unheard of, and Cramer could tell by that, how on edge he was.

"The man knows what he's doing," Cramer said. "Everyone says he's the best."

"I guess." Larkin still had a troubled frown on his face.

It was just a little over an hour before Buddy Farrell was back in Larkin's office, with the results of Danny's polygraph. He had a printout of Danny's reactions and he was prepared to go over it with the two detectives.

"What are you saying exactly?" Larkin asked.

"In my opinion the man is telling the truth," Buddy concluded. "He is not your shooter, nor does he know who pulled the trigger."

"Damn," Cramer exclaimed.

"So you're saying that he has no idea who hired him."

"I know it sounds crazy, but I asked the questions several different ways, and it always came out that he was telling the truth."

"Some people can beat these things, isn't that right?" Cramer asked.

"It is possible, but I don't think Danny Preston is one of them."

Larkin and Cramer knew Buddy Farrell's reputation and although they were disappointed with the results, they had to accept the man's conclusion.

"What about..."

"He doesn't have a clue as to who Cassie Thompson is. If you were hoping for a connection, there isn't any."

Cramer's eyes flew directly to Larkin's in time to see him breathe a sigh of relief.

"He has never met the woman. If there's nothing else, I'll gather my stuff and get out of here."

"I think that's all we need," Larkin said, pumping his hand in gratitude.

"You know it still doesn't prove anything," Cramer said at last. "If Danny is telling the truth he doesn't know who hired him."

That was true, and Larkin was back to feeling uneasy.

"Now what?" Cramer asked. "We can't book Preston for murder. We can't book him for kidnapping, because technically the woman was never kidnapped."

"We'll hold him for extortion for the time being," Larkin said. "I want to question him again about the family. He has a connection with one of them even though he's not aware of it. When I talk to him again, I'll bring up their names one by one until something clicks. If it doesn't happen with the family, we'll start with the help."

"You can relax a little now." Cramer grinned.

"What do you mean?"

"At least there isn't a positive link to your girl."

"Unless he knows her by another name?"

"Like I say. You're a trusting soul, aren't you?"

Larkin hoped he was wrong but there was a nagging feeling there was a connection between them. Maybe he felt that way because her gun was the murder weapon.

It was in the wee hours of the morning, while Larkin couldn't sleep, that he decided to make the trip to North Carolina. He and Cramer had put so much faith in finding the person with the mysterious DNA and it had been such a letdown when Danny Preston wasn't the murderer. Larkin had been so sure he was the key to solving the case and now they were back to square one. The answer had to be back where the past converged with the present.

About three in the morning, Larkin got out of bed, showered, and packed a few clothes. He sat down with his cup of coffee and began to look over his atlas. For the life of him, he couldn't remember the name of the town where Cromwell's wife had grown up.

Larry had mentioned it several times, but he really hadn't paid much attention. He looked at his watch again. It was too early to call Mr. Cromwell. *Who would know?* he wondered. He couldn't call Carrie Risner, especially at this time of the morning. He really wished that he didn't have to tell anyone what he was up to, but he had no choice. He would have to call Cassie. What was worse than calling someone he hauled in for questioning, but now having to ask her for help.

He figured if he drove down it would take him a good eleven hours. Maybe he could just start driving and call later from somewhere on the road. He didn't even know if he would find anything after he got there, but it was for sure he wasn't finding the answers here. The case was rapidly becoming cold and he refused to allow it to go unsolved.

About six o'clock he called Cramer, who was getting ready to go   to work, and told him his plans. Cramer assured him that he could handle going to court with Danny Preston and explaining the charges against him. He had already called Deets, explaining that he felt the need to investigate Julie Cromwell's family. Deets had been all for anything that would help solve the case. Now for the hard part; calling the woman who he had just made love to, the one he just dragged to the police station to question about her gun, and asking her for information when she might tell him to go to hell. He paused with his hand on the phone. He had to do it. He didn't know the name of the town he was going to, or the name of Julie's relatives. Maybe he could call James Risner, he thought, and then quickly decided against it. James had met Carrie after they had moved here, so he doubted he would know anything.

He braced himself and quickly dialed the phone. He wished he didn't have to alert any of the family of his planned trip, but he just couldn't head for North Carolina and check out every little rat hole until he found the right one. You just didn't pull into a strange town and go up to strangers looking for the man who molested both of his daughters twenty years ago.

The phone rang at least six times before a sleepy voice answered. "Someone better be dead, or at least sick."

"Cassie?"

"Karl?"

"I'm sorry to bother you, but I don't know where else to turn."

"Sorry, I'm not thinking too clearly. I was up all night doing rewrites. What can I do for you?"

"I need to know the name of the town in North Carolina where your dad is from."

"Do you want to know where Dad is from or where Julie grew up.?"

"They didn't live in the same town?"

"They lived in neighboring towns." Her voice wasn't too enthusiastic.

"Look, I know you're mad at me..."

"Not really. l know you're just doing your job."

"Still, I know you didn't expect me to act the way I did..."

"Because we went to bed together. This is modern times, Karl. People have casual sex all the time."

"It wasn't that way for me. I want you to know that."

"Don't worry about it, Karl, you don't owe me anything and I won't tell anyone. What happened between us is our business."

"Thanks. I don't have to tell you how much trouble I'd be in if Deets ever found out. I think he's fond on you. "

"Deets isn't my type. He wasn't when we were kids and he definitely isn't now."

Larkin didn't realize how relieved he would be to hear that. "I miss you," he said at last.

"I miss you too."

"Maybe I'll see you when I get back."

"The town my dad grew up in was Harrisburg. It's quite a bit bigger than Galvin, where Julie was from. Why?"

"I'm thinking about taking a little road trip," He said, thinking how grateful he was that he'd called her first. He had thought Larry called the town Garrison. He had found Garrison on the map and it had looked like a good-sized town. "How do you spell that?"

"Just like it sounds. G-a-l-v-i-n. "You must be desperate for a vacation, Karl."

"You know it's not a vacation."

"Do you think you'll find something there?"

"I really don't know. I'm finding nothing here."

"I would go with you if I wasn't on a deadline," she told him.

He didn't say so, but he didn't want her along. He wanted nothing to hinder him from doing what he had to do. On a personal note, he would have loved to have her along. "Maybe next time." He was only half joking. Maybe they could be together after they settled this thing. Once he knew she had nothing to do with the murder. He was thinking it, but he never said it.

"Is there anything else?"

"Yes, I need to know what Julie's dad's name is."

"His name is Nash Collins. I only heard his name mentioned once and it was right after my dad and Julie married. Julie was having a hard time with her pregnancy, and the doctor said it was because she had sex too young and it had messed up her insides. My dad didn't know that I was in the room, but I heard him say he could kill Nash Collins. I asked my dad later who that was, and he said it was Julie's father. I wondered why my dad was so mad at him, and he said because he had hurt Julie. That is all I know about the situation. I never asked any more questions because I knew it was a touchy subject with both of them."

At six-thirty, Larkin headed south. He wanted to talk to Cassie longer, but he needed to get to Galvin by Saturday morning. It was a little dot on the map and he would have to drive who knows where to find a place to stay. He planned to spend the weekend resting up, for he figured there would be little open, business-wise, and then start the first thing Monday morning. He wanted to find and interview people who knew the Collins family. If nothing else, he would scare Nash Collins by letting him know the child abuse was out in the open. If there was a link between what happened to Julie, as a child, and her murder, he would know it before he left Galvin.

Larkin had to drive fifteen miles further to the town where Larry grew up to find a place to stay. It was a small motel and if anyone left the light on for him, it must have been one of the giant water bugs which scampered across the floor when he turned on the light.

He had gone back to the office and told the heavyset woman working the desk there were cockroaches in his room big enough to put a saddle on.

The woman enjoyed a belly laugh at his expense and informed him that they weren't roaches, they were water bugs, and he might as well get used to them for everyone had them down here. When he told her he thought he ought to look for another place, she told him good luck, and that there wasn't another motel in fifty miles in any direction.

"What's the deal with all these bugs flying-united?" he asked.

She laughed again. "They're called love bugs, for obvious reasons."

"Humph," he snorted. He didn't care if she thought he was a snob. He was hot; he was hungry, and disgusted.

She went back to reading her book and he went back to his bug infested room.

He just hoped that the damned things stayed on the floor and didn't want to sleep with him.

Larkin got up about six o'clock and walked to a homey-looking little diner. A half-asleep waitress brought him a menu and set a cup of coffee before him. "Cream or sugar?" she asked automatically.

"Cream only," he said, taking the menu from her as she set down three little cartons. At first, Larkin thought the menu was a joke. It said "breakfast, lunch, and dinner."

"I guess it will be breakfast," he said, smiling and shrugging his shoulders.

"Good choice," the waitress answered, stifling a yawn. "How do you want your eggs cooked?"

"Scrambled will be fine," thinking to himself that it would be hard to mess up a scrambled egg.

"Bacon or sausage?"

"Bacon is fine."

"Toast or biscuits?"

"Toast, dry. I would like a little jelly if I could."

"Jelly comes with the toast. She looked at him as if he should have known. "You want gravy over your eggs?"

"No-Just plain." He wondered if these people had ever heard of cholesterol. He also wondered what happened to southern hospitality, but he kept it to himself.

Larkin studied her nametag. "Christy, are you familiar with the town of Galvin?"

"I should be. I've lived there for thirty years."

How lucky was he? "Do you know the Collins family?"

"The only Collins I know lived out in the country, about a mile out of town. You want anything else?" she asked, tapping her pad with the pencil.

Larkin looked around the diner. There was no one but him and the greasy-looking cook he could see behind the counter. It was not as if he was keeping her from something.

He ignored her rudeness and tried again. "How many in the Collins family?"

She hunched her shoulders. "People in this town mind their own business."

"They had two girls. One was named Julie and the other Carrie, does that ring a bell?"

"I didn't know either of them very well. We went to school together, but they were about five or six years ahead of me. They also had a younger daughter, but she died I think. Anyway, the oldest two girls left this town ages ago. Thought they were too good to live here, I heard. Look, I need to get back to work. Why are you asking all these questions?"

"Julie, the youngest girl was murdered. I'm the detective assigned to her case. I thought maybe her family might know something that would help me find her killer."

Christy looked surprised to hear of her death, but she told him, "Her family is all gone as far as I know. I think her old man passed away a few years back, and her mother is in the hospital somewhere. There is no one else that I know of."

"You said something about them having another daughter?"

"Yes, they had a girl that was younger than me."

Larkin felt disappointment hit him in the gut. He hoped the girl was wrong about the old man being dead. Larkin would like nothing better than to make him pay for hurting his children. There was also the horrible thought that there had been another daughter.

"What happened to the other girl, did you say?"

"She died. I don't really know how. Look, they lived out of town and we lived in town. They didn't socialize very much. You hear rumors, but you don't put much faith in them."

"What kind of rumors?"

"That the girl killed herself; that the parents might have been involved in some way. It's a small town; people talk."

"What did you hear about the other two girls?"

"That they thought they were too good for Galvin. I told you. I heard that Julie married a rich guy, and the other one went to live with her. All I know is they both left and I never saw them again. I heard they moved to another state."

"By the way, I'm Detective Karl Larkin." He offered to shake her hand. "Thanks for your help."

She seemed to think about it for a minute before she offered to shake with him. "I'm Midge Grover. My husband and I live in an apartment at the edge of town." She was frowning. "Do you think someone down here murdered her?"

"There are a few details I need to clear up, but I doubt that it has to do with anyone here." He didn't want the town people hearing of this and getting suspicious. Larkin knew in a place this small, people tended to stick together. If they became hostile toward him, he wouldn't find out diddle squat. "I just figured if I could talk to her family I might be able to get some insight on who might have killed her."

Christy eyed him curiously. "I hope you find out who did it," she said after a time.

"The Collins house, where is it located?" he asked as she started to walk away.

"It was torn down ages ago. Herb Smith bought the land to pasture his horses. Look, do you want those eggs or not?

"Yes, and thanks a lot for the information."

The woman didn't answer, only hurried away before he could ask anything else. A few minutes later, he saw her with the cook, their heads together and deep in conversation. They must have felt him eying them because they both looked up at the same time, then Christy turned her back and walked into the kitchen. It was only natural for them to be curious about him, he decided. His reason for being here would be all over town by tomorrow. That was all right. Every town had at least one gossip and he hoped he had found it.

People were starting to filter into the restaurant and Larkin's hope of talking to Christy when she delivered his food was fading fast. As slow as she was, she would never keep up.

His breakfast turned out to be decent, but he kept having visions of water bugs, that everyone supposed to have, running around over the grill. Boy, would he be glad to go home.

After breakfast, he planned to stop by the sheriff's office, for he had seen it while looking for a place to stay.

When Christy stopped to deliver his check, he asked her, "Does the sheriff work on Saturday?"

"Humph!" She sniffed. "That fat-assed blob will be in there, but working, I doubt it."

CHAPTER 17

---◆---

Larkin waited until Monday morning and with the help of the girl at the front desk, he rented a car to drive to the sheriff's office in Galvin.

The receptionist eyed him suspiciously. "Can I help you?" she said as he walked up to the desk.

"I need to see Sheriff Johnston," he read the name printed on the office door.

"Do you have an appointment?" The girl had worked for the man long enough to know that her boss never liked to do anything that wasn't necessary.

"I'm here on official business. I'm Detective Karl Larkin."

She hit the intercom button and awaited an answer. "Yes?" asked the irritated voice over the wire.

"There is a Detective Larkin here to see you. He says it's urgent."

After a time the crackly voice ordered, "Send him back."

Dale Johnston shifted his massive frame, causing his office chair to groan in protest. Taking a small coffee can from the side of his desk, he spit, and then moved the cud of tobacco over in his right jaw. Larkin's first thought was never to complain about Cramer's licking sugar off his fingers ever again. He didn't offer to shake with Larkin and that was just as well.

"You ain't from 'round here." It wasn't a question, but a statement... His milky blue eyes narrowed as he scrutinized Larkin.

"I'm from out of town," Karl admitted. He didn't feel that it was important to tell him that he was from out of state. "I'm investigating the murder of Julie Cromwell. She used to be Julie Collins; you may know her."

"Yeah, I know her. But her and her sister left Galvin years ago. I don't know what that has to do with us."

"Maybe nothing. Maybe everything," Larkin said. He was beginning to get a little peeved with the sheriff's lack of cooperation.

"Look," he moved his massive body closer to Larkin and squinted up at him. "All I know about the woman is she married some rich dude, left her family and this town and didn't look back."

"Do you mind if I sit down?" Larkin said, looking around for a chair.

"You can take a seat from the reception area," he said, pointing to a couple of wing-backed chairs outside his office door.

So much for small-town hospitality, Larkin thought, as he tried to hold the door and drag the chair at the same time. He shut the door behind him.

"I usually leave the door open, 'cause it gets stuffy in here,"

"I'd rather keep this private if you don't mind." Larkin wanted it closed and he knew there was no danger of the other man getting off his duff to open it.

"You don't have to worry about Betsy. I think the woman is brain dead." He smiled as though he had said something funny, showing brown uneven teeth. Larkin had the urge to run his tongue over his own teeth.

"I heard about her murder on the news. I wondered if it was old Nash's daughter."

"I would like to talk to her parents about their daughter, if you will just tell me where they live."

He smiled again showing his nasty teeth. "Ol' Nash is residing over at Shady Rest Cemetery."

"He's dead!" Larkin felt shock and disappointment. The waitress said she thought he had died, but Larkin was hoping it wasn't true. He wanted him to pay for his crimes.

"We ain't in the habit of burying them alive round here."

"What about his wife. Is she still alive?"

"She breathing, if that's what you mean. "She's in a place called Fairview. Crazy as a loon, they tell me."

"I would still like to talk to her," Larkin said, "if you will just give me directions."

"I'll give you directions, but she ain't talked in three years. Maybe a big-city cop like yourself can do something her doctors can't." He smirked at Larkin. Larkin was glad Cramer wasn't along. He was too hotheaded and even he himself would like to push the big blob off his chair.

"You say she doesn't talk?" Larkin asked.

"They can't get a word out of her, or so I hear. Not since that last girl of theirs hung herself."

Larkin swallowed. He was sure he was hearing about another victim. "How old was the girl when she died?"

"She was sixteen. What I want to know is what do you think the Collins had to do with their daughter's death?" His milky eyes had narrowed and he was getting upset about where the questions were leading.

"Look, I didn't say that the family had anything to do with this. I just thought that it might have something to do with her past. Is there anyone else in the Collins family I could talk to?"

"Judy's parents died when she was a girl. Nash's parents died in a car crash when my dad was sheriff in 1965."

"What about brothers or sisters, aunts, uncles?"

"There's no one left but crazy Judy and that oldest girl of theirs. I have no idea where she is. I think it broke the old man's heart when them two girls ran off like they did."

"I'll just bet it did." Larkin's sarcasm was out before he could think.

"What are you getting at?"

"Were there ever any allegations of child abuse against Nash Collins from anyone in this town?"

"No. Why?" His eyes narrowed. "Is there something you're trying to say, Mr. Larkin?"

"Only that both of the older girls claimed to have been sexually abused by their father." Larkin watched the sheriff closely for a reaction.

"Is that right? He shifted his weight, but made no other comment.

"Was there an investigation into the death of the younger girl?"

"I can assure you that the girl took her own life. I handled the investigation myself."

"Weren't you curious as to why a sixteen-year-old girl would want to kill herself?"

"Frankly, I thought maybe she might be as crazy as her mama." He gritted. "You ever think that they all might be nuts?"

"It's possible that the father caused all the problems, even with the mother. Did you ever think of that?"

"Just exactly what is your business here, besides making accusations against a dead man who can't defend himself?"

"I'm just looking for the truth," Larkin informed. "Where are the county records for Galvin kept?"

"The county seat is Harrisburg. I don't know if they have what you're looking for, but that is where the courthouse for this county is"

"Do they have a library?"

"Not a reader myself, so I can't help you there."

That revelation didn't surprise him. "Well, thanks, Sheriff. You've been a real help. I might see you again before I head home." Larkin's sarcasm was lost on the man.

As he started to leave, Johnston stopped him. "Would you mind putting your chair back? That way I won't have to get up."

"By all means," Larkin said, picking up his chair, dragging it along with him. The sheriff went back to chewing his cud.

CHAPTER 18

The courthouse was typical of any small town. Larkin was grateful that at least the girl working behind the counter had a smile on her face. That was probably going to change when she found out why he was here.

"I'm Detective Karl Larkin," he introduced himself as he stepped up to the counter, holding out his hand to shake with her. "I'm investigating the murder of Julie Cromwell, she used to be Julie Collins."

"My name is Dora Lancing," she said, taking his hand. "Yes, I heard about her on the news, but didn't she live somewhere in Ohio?"

"That is where I'm from." He waited for her face to change and was surprised when it didn't.

"It's a shame about her and her sister... "

"You know about her sister?"

"Yes. She killed herself, people say."

For a moment Larkin thought he had found someone who knew about Julie's and Carrie's abuse, but suddenly realized that she was talking about the youngest girl.

"Did you know the girl well, the one who killed herself?"

"Oh no. She was a lot younger than I was. She and my little sister were pretty good friends."

Larkin's ears perked up. "You don't say?"

"They were in school together."

"Did your sister ever say anything about any kind of abuse going on in the home?"

He knew he had hit pay dirt when Dora hung her head. "It was hinted at. I don't think Terry came right out and said it, but yes. Linda, that's my sister, thought so."

"Why didn't your sister tell someone; a counselor or a teacher?"

"Linda came to me for advice right before the girl killed herself. We were trying to decide what to do when the next thing we hear is that she was dead. Linda was distraught. She wanted to go to the police right then."

"Why didn't she?"

"Frankly, Mr. Larkin, I talked her out of it. The girl was already dead, and Linda and I had to live in Galvin. You're either one of the community or you're an outsider. If you make accusations against one of them, you had better be able to prove it. It was only Linda' word against his."

"I see," Larkin said.

"No, you don't see, Mr. Larkin. There are two kinds of people born in Galvin: The ones that leave, and the ones who will die there. My sister and I are the latter. Our family has lived in Galvin for generations."

Larkin shook his head. He did understand how unforgiving a small town could be. "Dora, there is a way you can help me after all."

"How is that?" she asked cautiously.

"I need to go over some records pertaining to the Cromwells, and the Collins."

She breathed a sigh of relief. "I'd be glad to help you with that. Just tell me what you need."

"I don't know exactly. I understand that Lawrence Cromwell lived around here when he was in school."

"Are you talking about the man Julie Collins married?"

"Yes, do you know him?"

"My older sister still raves about him, He was into sports. He lived right here in Harrisburg. He was the golden boy on the football team. They're big in sports here in Harrisburg," she explained. "Anyway, he won a scholarship to a school somewhere up North. He didn't take it though. He wound up getting married instead and going to school locally. His wife died, I think."

"She did," Larkin agreed. "That would have been Cassie's mother. I guess I'll just start by checking births, marriages, deaths, etc. Just bring me anything that you think will be of help."

"I'll be right back," the girl told him. "There is an unused office right across the hall," she said pointing. "You are more than welcome to use it. We usually need it for real estate closings, but there is nothing scheduled today."

"Thanks, Dora. You've been a big help, and yes, that will give me some privacy." He felt so grateful he wanted to kiss the woman. It was the most help he had gotten since he came to this state.

Dora loaded him down with files, and closed the door on her way out. In a few minutes, she was back with a couple of other folders. "These belong to the Cromwell children," she said and popped back out the door.

That would be Todd's and Tina's, Larkin thought. He could have sworn that Larry told him Tina had been born in Springfield. Maybe not, he thought as he began going through the backlog of information Dora had put before him.

She had brought him files dating back to the birth of Larry's parents. It was boring, but nothing popped as having to do with the matter at hand. Lawrence had a brother that was stillborn, and no other siblings. He had married the first time at the age of eighteen, to Kelly Blaine. That would be Cassie's mother, Larkin assumed. There was a death certificate for her dated a few years later. Lawrence had told him in one of their interviews that his parents had been rich and that they had supported him while he was in school. When he had married, the couple had lived with his folks so he was able to go on with his studies. He had quit school after his wife had become ill and after her death, he had waited a few years before going back and finishing his education. Larkin had just found out that Cassie had been born about seven months after the marriage, possibly the reason it was so hasty. He was learning more and more about the family's life, but nothing to indicate that something from the past had come back to haunt them. He was down to the children's folders and still nothing seemed to be amiss. Todd had been born soon after Julie and Lawrence had been married, but he already knew the story on that. He picked up the last folder, thinking it to be Tina's, and feeling disappointed that he had made this trip on a wild goose chase. He scanned it quickly, and then went back over it again. Mother's name Julie Cromwell; Father's name Lawrence Cromwell, baby boy unnamed. Adoptive parents blank. All other information concealed, and agreed upon by all parties involved. He read it all again then called Dora.

"It says here that Julie and Lawrence Cromwell had a child they must have given up for adoption, but there is no other information. What does all of this mean?"

"I have no idea. I'll get my supervisor and see if she can tell us anything."

Dora came back awhile later followed closely by a matronly woman who didn't look happy to have been disturbed.

"What can I do for you?" she said. Her eyes first sized up his appearance, then traveled to where Dora had piled stacks of files on the table. It was easy to see she didn't approve of him or the disarray he had left in his wake.

"I'm working on a murder case and I needed help finding some information missing from a file."

Dora introduced him to the woman, but Larkin could tell she wasn't impressed. She took the file and scanned quickly over it.

"What is it you need help with?" she asked impatiently.

"It says that Julie and Lawrence Cromwell had a baby they gave up for adoption, but it doesn't have the baby's name, or the couple who adopted him."

"That is because both couples agreed to conceal that information."

"How would I find out who adopted the boy?

"You can't, unless you're psychic. You see the lawyers' signatures here?" She pointed to the writing scrawled across the paper. "It was all set up legally by both parties, and the conditions were agreed upon."

"Would you know who they were?"

"No, I don't," she sniffed, "and if I did, I wouldn't tell you. I'd be breaking the law."

"Do you have any idea how I could find out? I feel it's really important to my case."

"You could ask Lawrence Cromwell," she said, walking away.

"I'm sorry," Dora said after she was gone. "The old crow thinks she owns this place, and she doesn't have the greatest personality, as you can see."

"Don't worry about it." He patted her shoulder. "Lawrence Cromwell and I have a pretty good relationship, and he wants to solve his wife's murder. I just thought if I knew the information while I was here, it might save me some trouble."

Larkin's mind had already jumped ahead. He would go straight to Larry when he got back and ask him. Maybe the boy had found out who his real parents were and felt they owed him money. He might be angry enough with his mother for giving him away that he killed her.

"Dora, do you think that your sister would talk to me about Terry Collins?"

"I don't see what help she could be at this point..." Dora hesitated. She was protective of her little sister. "Linda is very sensitive, and this has weighed heavily upon her..."

"Please. She may know more than she thinks. I need help in finding justice for both of these women."

Dora thought about it for a time, her forehead furrowing before she told him, "I'll call her. If she says she will see you, I'll get in touch."

"I'm at the motel down the street." He scribbled the number on a piece of paper and handed it to her. "I'd appreciate a call either way, because I plan on leaving for home sometime tomorrow."

"I'll call you," she promised before they parted company.

Larkin wondered if he would ever hear from Dora again. He supposed it was only natural for her to wonder what good it would do for him to talk to her sister. What could he do now that the girl and her dad were both dead? He guessed he just wanted someone to confirm there was abuse in the home. He had even asked for Dora's number, but she had refused, saying her husband was jealous and she didn't want trouble. Larkin didn't persist. The woman had helped him more than anyone else had, and the last thing he wanted to do was cause her trouble.

He called Cramer around four in the evening, telling him that he hadn't found much, but there might be one promising lead, which he would discuss with him when he returned home.

They had charged Danny Preston with extortion and fraud. The judge had set his bail at a hundred and fifty thousand dollars, assuring they would be able to hold him for a while, since the stolen money was safe in police custody. Larkin wasn't prepared to charge him with murder just yet, but who knows what later would bring. Keeping him safe in jail was the main thing at this point.

Larkin's phone rang about 5:00 and Dora Lancing was on the line. Her sister Linda was willing to talk with him the next morning at 9:00.

CHAPTER 19

---◆---

Linda Brown was not what Larkin expected. Where Dora was brunette and tall, Linda was a petite little blonde with an infectious smile. She welcomed Larkin enthusiastically into her well-kept home.

"I'm sorry I couldn't see you sooner, Mr. Larkin," she said as she led him into the front room and offered him a seat. "I needed to get my husband and children off for the day." He could tell by the way she handled herself; she took her duties as wife and mother seriously.

"That's fine, Mrs. Brown, is it?" He held out his hand to shake with her, which she accepted gladly.

"Please call me Linda. Mrs. Brown makes me feel old." She smiled, lighting her whole face. "Dora *said* you wanted to talk to me about Terry Collins." Her expressive face turned to instant sadness.

"Your sister said you and she were close friends."

"As close as she would allow us to be, I suppose. She was a very quiet person. Sad, is the way I would describe her. Would you like a cup of coffee, Mr. Larkin?"

The coffee smell was drifting over the house causing his mouth to water.

"If it wouldn't be too much trouble, I'd love one."

"It's no trouble at all," she said rising. "My husband isn't a coffee lover and I'm afraid I drink far too much during the day. How do you like it?"

"Just a little cream, if you have it."

In a few minutes, she was back with two steaming cups almost as big as the ones made for soup. "It's nice to have someone to share coffee with," she said.

"A girl after my own heart." He smiled as she placed the cup next to him on a coaster she retrieved on the way back from the kitchen. She was a person who took care of her modest possessions. Larkin admired that. He was beginning to have great deal of respect for Dora Lansing's little sister.

"That's good," Larkin praised after sampling the hearty brew.

"I get it too strong for most people, I'm afraid," she admitted.

"Being a policeman I have had a lot stronger."

Her face changed, bringing her back to the reason he was here. "Terry Collins didn't have any friends, except me. She was quiet and stayed to herself. I felt sorry for her and I made a point of seeking her out."

Larkin remembered her sister talking about Linda taking in strays. She was a very caring person and it came across in her personality. "Did she talk to you about her home life?" He felt directness was something that Linda Brown could relate.

"She didn't tell me straight out that the old monster was abusing her, if that is what you're asking. But I believe that he was." Her voice held a soft harshness, probably the closest she would ever come to raising her voice. No longer than he had talked to her, Larkin had a window into her character. Linda Brown would always root for the underdog: She would be there to help in time of trouble. It was probably the reason she had agreed to see him in the first place.

"What makes you believe he was abusing Terry?"

"Probable the same reason you believe he was abusing his other girls." She stared at him intently. "You do think he abused them, don't you?"

"Their husbands said that he sexually molested them," Larkin confirmed.

"Why didn't they try to help Terry?" she gasped, as if someone had knocked the wind out of her.

"I don't think they knew she existed," Larkin said truthfully. "They never talked about what happened. After they left, it was as if they wanted to deny it ever happened."

"I guess I can understand them not wanting to deal with it," she said.

"I think they tried, but it affected their everyday lives."

She shook her head. "Dora tells me that one of them was murdered?"

"Julie, the youngest."

"The next to the youngest," she corrected. "And you think it has something to do with her childhood?"

"I thought there might be a link to something in her past."

"But you don't know?"

"I can't really say," he admitted, "but it isn't looking too promising at this point." He took a drink of his coffee and lapsed into thought for a time.

Linda studied him before she spoke. "You're very troubled because of what happened to them, aren't you?"

He knew Linda Brown was very intuitive and a darn good listener. She would make a very good friend. "What happened in the past might not have been directly related to the murder, but I believe it was a contributing factor," he said at last. "You see, Julie made a pact with a known criminal to fake her own kidnapping."

"Why in the world would she do that?" Linda gasped.

"She did it to see if her husband loved her enough to pay a million dollars for her safe return."

"Oh my Lord!" Linda exclaimed. "Do you think the abuse left her unable to feel secure in her marriage?"

"I think so," Larkin agreed.

"That is so awful," Linda said, shaking her head. "That monster ruined all of their lives, didn't he?" She stared at Larkin waiting for him to confirm it.

He smiled. "You ought to have been a psychiatrist."

"I was thinking about it, but I got married and had children instead. Not that I've ever regretted it," she assured him.

"You would have made a good one," Larkin told her. He wasn't trying to flatter her. He felt the qualities were definitely there.

"What led you to believe that Nash Collins was abusing his daughter?"

"She would say things like she hated men because they owned their families, and they could do anything they wanted to, to them. You have to understand. She never came out and said there was anything going on. She was real evasive when I tried to pin her down."

"But you did get the feeling that something was going on."

"I could tell that she was afraid of him. One time they were at the general store in town and I was in there. Mr. Jennings, the store owner, made a comment on how pretty Terry was getting, and the old man put his arm around her. I could see her visibly cringe."

"Where was the mother during this?" Larkin burst out.

"You have to understand, Mr. Larkin. There is no women's lib in this town. His wife was uneducated, like half the women here. Families train their girls from childhood that the man is head of the house and what he says goes. The wife lets him do as he pleases and puts up with it," she said fiercely.

Larkin wondered if she was including herself in this, but he didn't ask. "So do you think that his wife knew about the abuse and looked the other way?"

"Probably. She was with them that day, but she never reacted. She walked around with her eyes averted, her head down, just like a zombie."

"So do you consider her a victim too?"

"Most definitely."

"When I came here, I had it in my mind to do everything I could to bring Nash Collins to justice. I can't tell you what a letdown is to find out he's dead." Larkin had shifted his weight so he could set down his cup. "It leaves a knot in the pit of my stomach to think he was never pay for his crimes."

"Do you believe in God, Mr. Larkin?" she said, staring directly at him.

He considered his answer for a second. "I was raised that way. I know my parents do. I'm not sure that I am convinced anymore."

"Well I do, Mr. Larkin." She pointed to the large Bible on the coffee table. "If that is God's-word and I believe that it is - there's a payday someday. I have to believe that Nash Collins is getting his." Her eyes held a sincerity that Larkin almost found comforting.

"I hope you're right, Linda, but I'm not counting on it. I believe in justice I can see," He said, rising and handing her his cup. "I'm just glad the bastard is dead and there won't be any more children he can destroy."

"Thank God for that," she said, rising also. "It was nice talking to you, Mr. Larkin, and I hope you find Julie's killer. I'm sorry I couldn't be of more help," she said as she followed him to the door.

"You were a great help," he assured. "Their husbands told me of abuse, but it never came from the women themselves. They just refused to talk about it. You confirmed for me that it was going on."

"I'll always believe so."

"I know that the other two women had all the signs of abuse. There had to be something horrible happening for a child of sixteen to take her own life."

At the door she said, "I take care of her grave, you know."

"That's very nice of you."

"'They stuck her off by herself, away from the rest of her family. It made me so sad."

"Why would they do that?" Larkin was angry.

"Her dad thought taking her own life brought shame to the family," she said. "How ironic is that?"

Larkin shook his head. "I'm just glad she had you," he said patting her arm.

"I did a fundraiser at church and the other ladies and I bought her a stone. I put flowers on her grave often, and when I go there, I often see other arrangements. Terry loved to garden and her dream was to own a nursery someday. The other women at church knew that, and they remember her by bringing flowers. I know she has the most beautiful garden in heaven."

Larkin knew it made her friend feel better to believe that, but all he could see was the ruined lives of three women. Cassie had asked him once if he had ever known anyone who deserved to die, and he had said no. He now had to eat those words.

The next day Larkin decided on going to Fairfield, a town he had to pass through on his way home. He felt he couldn't go home without trying to interview the mother.

He made one last stop on his way out of town. The flower shop was just before leaving the city limits. A beautiful potted lily caught his eye as he walked through the door. The color was between a pink and a purple and without thinking, he scooped it up and took it to the counter. The girl working assured him he had made a good choice. "My dad crossbreeds them," she told him. "He comes up with some awesome colors and fragrances sometimes."

All Larkin could think of was a girl lying dead, who would have loved to work in a place like this. He had bought the flower for her, and it was the first time he realized he was stopping by the cemetery on his way out of town.

He found her grave with no trouble after first running across a double plot marked for Nash and his wife, and surrounded by other members of the Collins family. Terry's grave was alone, like her life must have been. It was marked with a tiny stone paid for by Linda Brown and the ladies of her church. They were good people to remember a girl not related to them. Just when he was on the verge of losing faith in humanity decent folks like Linda brought it back.

It was a beautiful place, if you considered cemeteries in that way. Larkin had never liked them. He guessed it was because they testified to his immortality. The breeze swayed the trees gently, causing a peacefulness he couldn't explain.

"I've brought you a flower," he found himself talking to a grave, and wondering if he was crazy. As he placed the pot against the stone, a feeling passed over him. A warm breeze caressed his face and he felt Terry Collins knew why he was here and that she liked the flower.

"Get hold of yourself," he said aloud. This case was causing him to lose his mind.

Fairview was a place for the criminally insane. The graveyard had been tranquil, but there was no peace within these walls.

A nurse, who looked like she could kickstart a 747, led the way to where Judy Collins sat in a wheelchair. The woman's eyes stared straight ahead, blinking now and then from reflex. Her head lolled to one side, spittle draining from the corner of her mouth.

"Is she like this all the time?" Larkin asked Nurse Hatchet. That's the name he thought of when he saw her.

"I tried to tell you," the nurse sniffed. "She hasn't done a thing different since she came here three years ago. She doesn't say anything, and she doesn't do anything. She wears pampers and we change her like a baby."

"She must eat," Larkin observed. The woman was thin, but she didn't look starved.

"We put it in her mouth. Sometimes she swallows and sometimes she lets it run back out..."

"Is it alright if I try talking to her? I don't want to do anything to upset her."

"Knock yourself out," she told him. She handed him a little metal bell. "Ring this when you're ready to leave. I have other patients to care for, and I have to keep a watch. Sometimes she slides out of her chair and lies on the cold ground."

Larkin sat awhile watching the woman, wondering how he should start. Her expression never changed and she didn't move. The person who used to live here had gone. Without a word, he picked up the bell and rang it. It was time to go home.

CHAPTER 20

———◆———

Cramer was as glad to see Larkin as he was to be home. Larkin spent the evening telling him about the people he had met in Galvin and what he had found out about the Cromwells giving away a child.

"Maybe the kid grew up and found out his mother, who had given him away, was rich. Maybe he thought the Cromwells owed him money. He could have hated her enough to kill her."

Larkin had thought the same thing. People were murdered for less. It was definitely an avenue they needed to explore.

Larkin called Lawrence as soon as he arrived in town and asked for a meeting. The only other person who knew about the boy was dead. The answers had to come from him.

Lawrence sounded weary on the phone, but he had agreed to see Larkin. He opened the door wearing a nice suit; his hair looked recently cut. "Are you going out?" Larkin wondered if he had caught him at a bad time.

"I was working on a deal before all of this happened. I've since changed my mind and I was going today to cancel it."

"What kind of deal?"

"I had planned on building a strip mall just for an investment. I want to do something entirely different now. Anyway, I'm not interested in the same land as before."

"Did you back out of the deal before Julie died?" Her murder might have something to do with a deal gone bad.

"No, no. It's nothing like that. I haven't even spoken to the man yet. He doesn't know that I've changed my mind."

"I just got back from Galvin, North Carolina," Larkin blurted and waited for his reaction.

"Cassie said that you were going," he admitted. "I don't expect you found much. Our life has been here for years."

"There was one thing that interested me, Larry."

"And what was that?"

"That you and your wife gave a child up for adoption."

This time there was a reaction. "Yes, we did," he said, hanging his head. "Those records were supposed to be sealed."

"The files are closed, but I need you to tell me who the couple is that adopted the boy and where he is right now."

"I can't see any reason to do that. It has no bearing on the case."

"I would like to be the judge of that," Larkin said.

"I promised I would never tell."

"I know you're anxious to find your wife's killer, and it could have something to do with it."

"That's highly unlikely."

"I still need to know. What if the boy grew up and found out that you and your wife gave him away? He might have decided that you owed him something. Maybe he made friends with your wife and they arranged this kidnapping scheme. Maybe he hated her for giving him away. Hell-maybe he hated you both."

Lawrence held up his hand to stop him. "We gave the baby to Carrie and James Risner. The boy is Toby," he said at last. "Now do you see how crazy your whole theory is?"

"It was Toby you gave away?" Larkin was in shock.

"I'm not proud of it." Larry had stood up and began to pace. "You know the story on Todd. He was born right after Julie and I were married. I knew whom he belonged to, but I didn't care. I just was so glad to get her away from that man. Not long after Todd was born,

Julie began her first affair. I knew about it but I didn't want to lose her so we tried to work it out. When she told me she was pregnant, I was sick. The worst part was she didn't know if the baby belonged to her lover or me. I was a young man trying to get my practice started and Julie was having problems adjusting to being a mother and a wife. She cried and told me there was no way she could handle taking care of two kids. Frankly, I wasn't crazy about raising another child that wasn't mine. We were both a mess over it, so when she came to me and told me that Carrie and James were willing to take the baby; it seemed like the perfect solution for all concerned."

"Why was it a good solution for the Risners?"

"Carrie desperately wanted a child and she was unable to have one. You see, she became pregnant when she was too young, because of that father of hers, and it messed up her insides. She lost the child she was carrying and it left her unable to have other children."

It was slowly dawning on Larkin that Carrie had told him a lie. The story about her having an affair with Larry wasn't true. Still, Larkin had to know for sure. "I have something I have to ask you. When we found out that Toby was really your son, I confronted Carrie and she said the two of you had had an affair. Is that true?"

Lawrence was beginning to get a troubled frown on his face. "Carrie had feelings for me, but I have never been untrue to Julie."

"I suppose she only told me that to keep me from learning what really happened."

"You said that you found out that Toby was really my son. What did you mean by that?"

"When we tested his DNA that was when we knew he was your biological son."

"That's impossible."

"What do you mean, that's impossible?"

"We had a blood test done on the child at birth. If the boy had been mine, I would never have agreed to give him away." Larry's voice had risen. "The doctor who did the test said that he was ninety-nine percent sure he wasn't mine."

"I'm afraid he was wrong," Larkin said softly. "DNA doesn't lie. Who was the other man that your wife was having an affair with?"

Larkin seemed to recall Carrie telling him something about her sister being involved with a doctor.

"Oh my God-Oh my God." Larry was running his hand through his hair, completely agitated.

"By any chance, was the doctor who did your son's blood test the one she was having an affair with?"

"I found out later that he was." He was shaking his head. It was slowing dawning on him how completely he had been deceived.

Lawrence let loose a string of curses that Larkin wouldn't have believed him capable of, and slammed his fist into the wall. Never could the detective ever remember seeing someone so angry. He allowed the man to get it all out and then he asked, "Are you alright?"

Ignoring the question, he hissed through clinched teeth. "I can't believe I let those two trick me into giving away my own flesh and blood"

"You mean your wife and the doctor."

"I mean Julie and her sister. Carrie had to know the baby was mine, or she wouldn't have lied about the two of us having an affair. Julie probably blackmailed the doctor into it. She probably threatened to tell his wife about the affair." His voice held a hard note that Larkin had never heard before when he discussed his wife. At this moment, Larkin could see the hatred in his eyes. Maybe he could have killed her, Larkin thought.

Carrie knew all right, but he hoped Lawrence wouldn't do anything rash. "What do you plan on doing about the situation?"

Larry seemed to calm slightly. "I don't really know at this point."

"All I ask is that you think about it before you take action." Larkin felt responsible for opening this can or worms. He didn't know what he would do in a situation like this. He also wondered about Larry's mental attitude. He had found out that Larry could become violent. If his wife could do something like this to the man she claimed to love, he felt she was capable of anything. Maybe Larry had found out something that caused him to kill her. Larry hadn't known about Toby, because his reaction had been too real, but maybe she had done something worse.

"Do you think that James knew?" Larkin wondered.

"I doubt it," Larry volunteered. "He's a pretty decent guy, really. He is sort of like me. He is always walking on eggs to keep peace in the home."

Larkin shook his head. He had seen that in the man. He had probably been deceived, also.

"You don't really think it was Toby, do you?" Lawrence asked.

Larkin thought for a second. "I doubt it. The boy seems well adjusted and happy with his parents."

"Who he thinks are his parents," Larry corrected.

"At any rate I don't think he's the one."

"Where do we go from here?" Larry wondered.

"I haven't told you we found the mysterious donor of the DNA, have I?"

"That's great! Who is he?" Larry exclaimed.

"A man named Danny Preston. Do you know him?"

"I've never heard of him, but don't you think he killed Julie? Why is it you're still suspicious of the family?"

"He passed a lie detector test, for one thing. He admits to helping your wife with the fake kidnapping, and he even admits to attacking her in her car. He said she bit him and he hit her in the mouth to make her turn loose. She tried to bite him again and he hit her a glancing blow, cutting her head. His story coincides with the evidence found in her car. He says he went there as they planned and saw her waiting in her car. He remembered how attractive she was when he delivered the ransom note, and decided to make a play for her. She fought him like a wild cat (his words), and then she jumped from her vehicle and ran. We think his blood we found on the dashboard came from where your wife bit him. In the scuffle, he left a smudge on the car."

"Why isn't it likely that he also shot her?"

"There are several reasons that make me feel that he didn't. For one thing, he confessed that he is deathly afraid of guns."

"And you don't think he would lie? Look what a scam the man was involved in."

"When you have interviewed as many criminals as I have, you develop an instinct for knowing when someone is lying. He also passed the polygraph we gave him."

"What does he say about someone else being involved?" Lawrence looked him directly in the eyes.

"This is going to sound far-fetched to you, but he says that he received a phone call from someone he didn't know if this person had a weird voice that he didn't recognize. I think from the way he described it, that the person used a distortion device. Anyway, they explained that it was a fake kidnapping and that he would be paid five hundred thousand dollars.

"This guy has always been into petty crime. I don't see him getting involved in a murder," Larkin said.

"You're right. It does sounds pretty far-fetched."

"It's just crazy enough to be true," Larkin told him.

"You said he passed a lie detector test."

"Yes, he did."

"Can't those things be faked?"

"It has been done."

"Isn't it true the results can't be used in court?"

"That is also true, but I have found that most criminals can't fool them."

"But it has been done?"

Larkin had to nod his head.

"So where does that leave us?"

"We have tried to find the money. All we have is the money we took from Danny. There was a little over four hundred thousand dollars that hasn't been touched. There isn't a trace of the other half, which also leads me to believe there is someone else involved."

"Couldn't it just be that he has all the money, and he separated it in case he got caught?"

"That is indeed possible," Larkin agreed.

"But you don't think so."

"No, I don't. I don't believe he's that smart."

"What will you do now?"

"When I leave here, I plan to interview Danny Preston again. There has to be a connection between him and the person who hired him."

"I thought my wife hired him."

"I believe she went through a third party, like Danny said."

Larry looked skeptical. "I think you have the right man, Detective, and I think he acted alone."

Larkin made no other comment. The man had been through more than anyone he knew, and just when he thought it couldn't get worse, it did. He was afraid that now that the truth was out about Toby it would cause a bigger rift in the family.

"Sorry to be the bearer of bad news, yet again," Larkin apologized. They had gone to the door because Larkin was ready to leave.

Lawrence shook hands with him. "I'm glad to know the truth."

"I hope you and the Risners are able to work this out without messing up the boy." Larkin was worried.

"Carrie just wanted a baby so badly she went along with the scheme. She could have had children of her own if that father of hers hadn't messed her up. James does anything he can to make her happy. I blame that old man for most of this."

Larkin shook his head, because he blamed the man for all of it.

"Besides, Julie had a way of getting what she wanted. She would have threatened, sweet talked, and connived, whatever it took. I loved her, but I suffer no illusions about how she was. I feel stuck. I doubt there is anything I could legally do at this point. I did sign papers giving him to the Risners. I would have to prove that I didn't know he was mine. And how would Toby feel about me trying to take him from the parents he's known for all these years?"

"I see what you mean," Larkin said.

"I plan to think about it for a while before I do anything."

Larkin left for the office assured that Lawrence would do the right thing. What a predicament this poor guy had. The man must have a black cloud following him around. No one should have that kind of luck, or a wife who was his worst enemy.

The only thing Larkin knew to do at this point was to discuss the case with Cramer, and maybe talk with Danny Preston once more. There had to be a link between him and someone in the family or someone who worked for the Cromwells. He just had to pick his brain until he came up with whom.

Back at the office, Larkin told Cramer what he had learned from his interview with Larry. He made mention of how violent Lawrence had become about the betrayal.

"Damn," Cramer said, taking his usual spot on the corner of Larkin's desk. "Sounds like a motive for murder to me. I don't blame the man for popping her. Maybe we can get the charge reduced to manslaughter. He and the DA are friends, remember?"

"You still think it was Cromwell then?"

"Who else, bro? Look at what she did to him."

"He didn't know about Toby until I told him, I'm sure of that."

"Who knows what else the woman has done to him," Cramer said.

"Did you check all the phone records like 1 asked?"

"I've gone through all of the employees' phone records at Cromwell's practice. I've been unable to tie any of them to Danny Preston. I've checked Cassie Thompson's, her publisher's, editor's, and even her agent's phone records. I found nothing incriminating.

"I checked Danny's phone calls," Cramer continued. "Guess what I found?"

"I hope it's a lead at this point."

"It's more questions than answers, I'm afraid."

"What do you mean?"

"In tracing the incoming calls, I came up with two or three calls from the same number. It was about in the period in question, so I checked them out. All at phone number is from a house in a swank neighbor hood on the east side. It seems odd for someone like Danny to know anyone from there, so I went to check it out."

"Who lives there?"

"The Davidsons. They're supposed to have made money in printing. I went there to question them, but the house looked empty. The neighbors said they are both retired and they spend their winters in Florida. The neighbors seem to think they aren't back yet. No one has seen anyone around there for a while. The lady next door said that Mrs. Davidson usually has someone come in every now and then to check on things. Do you think that someone used their phone to hire Danny Preston?"

"That's exactly what I think."

"So, whoever contacted Danny about the fake kidnapping did it from that number."

"I wonder if the Davidsons know the Cromwells, by any chance," Larkin said.

"How would we go about finding out?"

"You need to take a trip over to Davidson Printing. Do you know where it's located?"

"It's not the tiny little place on the corner of Water and Main, where you take your life into your own hands when you pull into it?" Cramer asked.

"There have been a few accidents at the location, I believe."

"I wouldn't have thought a tiny place like that would make any money."

"See if the manager has a phone number where we can reach the Davidsons in Florida."

"You've got it. Anything else?"

"Don't ask too many questions. I don't want anyone to get word that we are investigating the Davidsons."

"We don't want to give the culprit a heads up that we are on to them. Right?"

"Just tell the employees that we are investigating a break-in and we need their number or at least the person to contact in case of emergency. We might get lucky and the Davidsons give us the person who has access to their house."

"That's a good idea, but do you think it's wise to lie?"

"It's not a lie. We're always investigating a break-in. You don't have to say it was the Davidson place."

Cramer stared at him for a second.

"What?" Larkin asked.

"You have changed since you started working on this case."

Larkin smiled. "Just go, will you? I need to interrogate Preston again."

"Okay. But if I get into trouble for lying, you had better go to bat for me."

"Break a leg."

"Same to you, partner."

"Oh, and by the way, Cramer. I think we're right on the verge of solving this case."

CHAPTER 21

"He what!" Larkin exploded on the young officer who he had asked to bring Danny downstairs for questioning.

Mark Bailey, a rookie just hired by the department, looked scared "Yes, sir," he said hesitantly. "He made bail just before you came back to the office."

Larkin didn't give him time to explain, only wheeled around and headed toward Bill Clayton's desk. He, like everyone else, tried to avoid old gloom-and-doom Clayton, but he was just upset enough to deal with him today.

No one around the precinct ever asked how he was, because people knew he would release enough negative vibes to affect the atmosphere for days. He had a feeling that is why Deets assigned him the job and set his desk over in the corner. All he had to do was handle the bail-making process. It was a great setup really. The man had never been a great beat cop, and it kept him out of everyone's hair. Clayton was usually good at the job, except for today, Larkin decided.

Clayton was his usual grumpy disheveled self, and even though it was going on ten o'clock, he yawned as if he was still half-asleep.

"I heard you let Danny Preston walk," Larkin barked.

"He made bail." Clayton shrugged. "That's what I do when they make bail," he said, shuffling through the clutter on his desk. Normally Larkin itched to organize the mess; today he itched to slap the big dope's face.

"He was under a 150,000-dollar cash bond."

"I'm aware of that."

"Someone paid it for him?"

"Yes."

"Who does Danny Preston know with that kind of money?"

"She said she was his wife. She gave me a certified check for the entire amount."

"You didn't question where she got the money?"

"It ain't none of my business where she got the money."

Larkin was furious. The man had to know what kind of a case they were working on, and to let someone like Danny Preston just waltz out without even questioning it was unbelievable.

He was angry with Clayton, but he was angrier with himself. He should have added more charges, and he should never have gone to Galvin when he did. He had been in such a hurry to leave he hadn't thought it through. Since they had Danny's share of the money he had believed there was no way he could make bail. What was wrong with his mind, falling for a story about some crazy voice on the phone hiring Danny? He was obviously in it with his wife, who had the other half of the money. "Damn," he said aloud as he thought about it. How could he have been so stupid? He had assumed that Danny had a connection to the Cromwell family, and it was his wife instead. The two of them were probably long gone with the rest of the money by now.

"What did she look like?" Larkin demanded.

"I don't know. She was forty maybe. Blonde-wearing sunglasses and a scarf. She handed me a check and told me she had to go because she was late for work. She said for Danny to take a cab home."

"Excuse me, sir." Larkin wheeled to see the young cop who had first told him of Preston's release. "I think she was wearing a blonde wig."

"Why do you say that?"

"I could see a wisp of darker hair at the neck line when she pulled the scarf higher up on her head. The scarf looked too small and she kept adjusting it, trying to cover all of her hair."

"Thanks," Larkin said. The kid was observant. He had the makings of a good police officer.

"I need their address," Larkin barked.

"Just keep your shirt on. I have his folder here someplace. I haven't had time to put it away."

What a shock, Larkin thought as he watched him shuffle through one stack of folders and start on another.

"Here it is..."

Larkin snatched it from him and quickly found the address. "Will you tell Cramer where I've gone? He should be back anytime."

"Sure. I have nothing to do but sit around watching for Cramer."

"I'll keep an eye out for him, sir." It was the rookie again.

"Give him this address." Larkin pointed to the one in the folder. Mark shook his head at Larkin, who was halfway to the door.

The house was on old two-story with lots of rooms. It held four separate apartments, two up and two down. Karl was looking for the house number as he was getting out of the car. Apartment 141 A was on the left, and there was a world of difference in appearance to side B. The other apartment had a broken window, repaired by nailing a board over the opening. Larkin lad to step over several discarded toys to get to the area in front of the Preston apartment.

Someone had swept away the leaves and debris from the other side and there was a welcome mat in front of the door. There were even frilly little curtains at the windows. It spoke of someone who was forced to live in poverty yet was trying to better themselves. Larkin always noticed how people lived. It spoke volumes about their character. Maybe because Danny Preston's wife craved nicer things, she went along with this crazy scheme.

The woman answered the door, drawing her tattered robe closer around herself as she faced the brisk May wind. She had washed her hair and rolled it up in a towel, but Larkin caught sight of blonde hair at the neckline. Larkin remembered Mark saying she was wearing a blonde wig. He must have been wrong, Larkin thought. He found himself looking around for Danny. He was just glad he had caught them before they could get away.

"Can I help you?" The woman was frowning as she noticed Larkin casing her apartment. She was looking at him, sizing him up, thinking he might be looking for someone in the next apartment. After noticing how well he was dressed she decided that wasn't the case.

"I'm Detective Karl Larkin. I'm looking for Danny Preston. May I come in?"

He flashed his badge and she stood aside for him to enter. Walking to the coffee table she found her cigarettes and lit up, inhaling before she spoke, "What's that little worm done now?"

Larkin stared at her. She was an attractive woman, or at least she had been. She now wore the hard look of a woman whose life had dealt her a bad hand.

"I beg your pardon," Larkin was confused. "Are you talking about your husband?"

Wasn't she aware he knew she had bailed Danny out of jail?

"My soon-to-be ex-husband. Isn't that who you're talking about? You said you were looking for Danny."

She waved Larkin toward a chair, and he took another quick glance around before sitting down. The place was shabby and bare, but it was shining clean.

"I don't understand," he said at last. "Didn't you just bail him out of jail?"

"Me!" she exclaimed. "If that man was in the proverbial jug with the lid on it, I wouldn't unscrew it to give him air."

"If it wasn't you, then some woman claiming to be you just paid his fine and he walked. Do you have any idea who... "

"Maybe one of his girlfriends. Hell, I don't know who he hangs around with. You can rest assured it wasn't me." She noticed Larkin looking around and laughed.

"You think he's here. I haven't seen the bastard since I filed nonsupport on him two months ago. What did he do, anyway, extort some little old lady out of her life earnings?"

"We have evidence that he is involved in a case of kidnapping and murder."

She gasped. "Are you talking about Julie Cromwell, the plastic surgeon's wife?"

"The very same."

"I heard they had arrested someone in connection with that, but they didn't give the person's name. The news said it was because they hadn't charged him yet. That was Danny?" She was staring at Larkin as thought she couldn't believe it.

Larkin nodded his head.

"You're wrong, Mr. Larkin. Danny is a con man, but he isn't a killer. He might try to rape some woman, even beat them up... "

"A wife never believes that their husband is capable of something like this."

"The paper said she had been shot. I know that Danny never shot anyone. I lived with the little snake for twelve years and he would never consider committing a felony of this magnitude. He was into petty crime and he always bragged about how smart he was not to get into anything where he could get serious prison time..."

"A million dollars is a big incentive, don't you think?"

"I know the money would have been a temptation, but I still say he wouldn't have gotten into something this big."

"I went over his file when we arrested him. I saw that you had him arrested for battery. He also assaulted Julie Cromwell in her car. Don't you think the violence could have gotten out of hand?"

"He beat me up more than once and he thought he was going to start doing the same to Cindy, that's when I called the cops."

"Mrs. Cromwell had been beaten and her clothes were torn. She had Danny's skin and hair under her nails. He admitted to assaulting her."

"I can see him being involved in the extortion, I can concede of him assaulting her, but someone else shot the woman," she said emphatically.

"Why do you say that?"

"Danny was deathly afraid of guns. If someone had one near him, he would come unglued. It was because of his childhood. His older brother was playing with his dad's gun. First, he pointed it at Danny and pulled the trigger and it didn't go off. Then he pointed at his twelve-year-old sister and pulled the trigger again. The gun fired and she went down. She died instantly. Danny would get pale and shaky just talking about it." She kept nervously glancing at her watch.

"Am I keeping you from something?" Larkin asked at last.

"It's just that I have to be at work soon."

"I'll try to make this fast. Did you or Danny know any of the Cromwells?"

"The closest I've ever gotten, is seeing Dr. Cromwell's commercial on TV."

"Do you know whether Danny knew any of them?"

"I doubt it. We didn't exactly travel in the same circles."

"I'm trying to establish a connection between Danny and the family. We believe Julie Cromwell hired him to set up a fake kidnapping. She wanted to see if her husband would pay to get her back. What we can't figure out is how she became acquainted with Danny."

"Who knows? He was like any other rat. He turned up anywhere there was a tasty morsel."

"Have you ever heard him mention Cassie Thompson?" He held his breath and awaited her answer.

"Not that I can recall. Who is she anyway?"

"She's Mr. Cromwell's daughter from another marriage. Her gun killed Julie. The odd thing is she reported the gun stolen three years ago."

"If he knew her, he never mentioned it to me."

It proved nothing that Dora had never heard of her, yet Larkin couldn't help feeling relieved.

"The money would have tempted Danny, all right."

"What about you, Mrs. Preston?" Larkin asked abruptly. "Would the money have tempted you? Are you afraid of guns?"

She burst out laughing. "You think I'm in this with him." It was dawning on her why Larkin was here.

"He had an accomplice. A half million would let you and your daughter live pretty well."

"I have to agree that it would have been tempting. Strippers don't have retirement plans. I work every day doing a job I hate just to keep our heads above water. Rest assured; Danny didn't offer me a deal. Me and his kid is the last thing on his mind."

"Mommy," a little blonde girl came from the next room, rubbing the sleepy out of her eyes, and peering cautiously at Larkin. She skimmed past him and headed for her mother's outstretched arms. "Honey, this is Detective Larkin. He's just here to ask Mommy a few questions." Dora stared at Larkin over the top of the girl's head. "She's everything to me. I scrimp and save just to put a roof over our heads. I take my clothes off for a living. I don't like dirty old men pawing me, but it's what I'm qualified to do. You might not believe me, but if I had my way, I would be making cupcakes and heading up the PTA. If Danny would help me just a little," her eyes filled with tears, "our lives would be so much better. You can rest assured, Mr. Larkin, that I would never do anything that would take me away from my little girl. I'm all she has."

Larkin only shook his head. He believed her. "So, you have no idea who would bail him out of jail?"

"Mommy, I'm hungry." The little girl squirmed on her mother's lap.

"I'm sorry, but I'm going to have to feed my daughter and get ready for work. My sitter will be here any minute."

"Go ahead and get your daughter some lunch. We're almost done here anyway. Do you have Danny's address?"

Dora had gone to the kitchen, which was really an extension of the living room.

"Let me guess. He gave my address as his."

"That's true," Larkin said, shaking his head.

"He lives in a dump, clear on the other side of town. He thought it would look better for him if he said he lived here with us."

Larkin noticed when she opened her cabinet it contained a loaf of bread, and the refrigerator contained a gallon of milk and a few eggs. The only other thing he saw was a jar of peanut butter and jelly combined.

Looking up from spreading the mixture on the bread, she told him, "The little weasel has never lived here with us. Oh, he used to come here all the time asking for money, but I haven't seen him lately. I figured it was because I kept turning him down."

"You were going to give me his address."

She rattled it off and kept on working, getting a plate and pouring the girl a glass of milk.

"You said you filed non-support for your daughter. Does that go through children services?"

"No. Probate court handles it. Why?"

"It's just that Julie Cromwell's sister works for children services."

"What's her name?"

"Carrie Risner."

"Oh, yes, I do know her. She was our case worker when I took Danny to court for abusing Cindy and me."

"How did you like her?" Larkin wasn't fond of the woman himself, but he would like to know how other people felt.

"She was great with Cindy," Dora called from the kitchen. "The court assigned her to be our family counselor."

"How did Danny get on with her?"

"Oh, you know Danny." She had finished with lunch and walked back into the living room, leaving her daughter to eat her sandwich. "He showed up for sessions just enough to keep him out of jail."

"How did she feel about Danny?"

"It's like everyone else that meets him. It doesn't take long to realize he's as useless as tits on a bull."

Larkin smiled at her colorful expressions. It was too bad Cramer wasn't along. They seemed to speak the same language.

"So, Danny wasn't so faithful at making his counseling sessions."

"No. At first, Mrs. Risner tried working with us as a family, but Danny wouldn't cooperate. After a while she just seemed to forget about him and concentrate on Cindy and me. She really helped us. Cindy became quite fond of her, as a matter of fact."

Larkin did feel that Carrie would be good at her job. The woman would certainly identify with an abused child.

"Do you still go for counseling?"

"Oh no. The sessions were over months ago." Again, Dora looked at her watch. "I'm sorry, but I do have to get ready for work."

Larkin headed for Danny's apartment, going over his conversation with Dora in his mind. He really felt bad for people who struggle all their life. Dora Preston would be the kind of person who would make use of a break. The trouble was, people like her seemed to go through their entire life without one.

There was something niggling at his mind. It was the same feeling he had every time he saw Toby Risner; until he had figured out it was his resemblance to Lawrence Cromwell. What was it that Dora Preston had said that had set the wheels turning again?

On his way to Danny's apartment Larkin called Cassie. He just felt the need to talk to her. He told her about Danny Preston and his wife, Dora, and their beautiful little girl living in poverty. He told her about Carrie Risner working with the family because of the domestic abuse. He told her he was on his way to see Danny once again to try to find a connection with her family.

It wasn't like Larkin to talk so much on his cell phone, but after talking to Cassie, he called Cramer, who was on his way back to the station. They were well into the conversation when something clicked in Larkin's brain.

"Oh my God!" he exclaimed. "I know who killed Julie Cromwell. Just get over to 32 Mary Street, and hurry," he told Cramer. "I don't have time to explain." He threw the phone on the seat and began to accelerate.

The woman who bailed Danny out of jail wasn't a friend. She intended to kill him. He hoped to make it in time to save his life.

CHAPTER 22

———————— ◆ ————————

Danny Preston never stopped to think until he was in the cab headed home. The police had told him that his wife had paid his bail. That didn't make sense, but he wasn't going to worry about it until he was a long way from anything to do with the police station.

Why would a woman who hated his guts pay $150,000 to get him out of jail, and better still, where would she get that kind of money?

In a flash, something reached inside his chest and squeezed his heart. He had never known fear like this before. It enclosed him like a shroud. Dora didn't bail him out. It was the killer. She was afraid he would give her away. Now she was going to kill him, shoot him down as she did Julie Cromwell. He remembered those bone-chilling phone calls that threatened his life if he didn't stay out of trouble.

How he wished he'd listened closer to the distorted voice. He should have paid more attention, but his attention span wasn't that long. When that vibrating, weird-sounding voice had offered him a half million dollars, the money was all he could think about. He laid his head back against the seat, letting it roll back and forth, trying to clear it. What else had the voice said? He needed to think.

"Oh my God," he said aloud to himself in the back of the cab. That person, the one that had not been real to him at the time. It had told him to stay out of trouble. It had told him not to lead the police to them or he was a dead man. Whoever the psycho was, they would do it, too. He had read how she shot Julie Cromwell through the heart, but wasn't satisfied; she had put one in her brain also. That was about to happen to him too. The thought made him shiver.

The three-story apartment building was on the south end, far from the Cromwells of the world. In the daytime little dirty kids, both black and white, ran barefoot over the barren ground that served as lawn. It was early spring, but it didn't stop the parents from letting their little brats run around half-naked. For some reason he thought of his own daughter. Her mother spoiled the little brat, but at least she put clothes on the kid.

The cab pulled up to let him out. There was a drug deal going down on the corner. He had learned early to look the other way, and after the fake kidnapping, he had dreamed of using the money to move to a decent neighborhood. Maybe there was still a way to do it. He could promise a lawyer a chunk of the money if he could prove he had done nothing wrong. All he had done was make a deal with Julie Cromwell to do a fake kidnapping. He had earned that money. He had done what he was supposed to do and it was his pay. He couldn't help it if someone had killed her. That was who the police should hold accountable, not him.

The elevator jerked and rumbled as it started its ascent, coming to rest on the third floor with a loud thump. Every time he used the thing, he wondered if it was going to make it to the top.

The hallway was dim and stretched endlessly toward his apartment. Half of the light bulbs had burned out and the others must be forty watts. A killer could be just beyond the elevator door and it's doubtful that he would be able to see them.

He tensed as a mouse scurried across the floor in front of him-at least he hoped it was a mouse. He hurried to apartment thirteen and tried the door. The door remained locked, which meant no one had broken in. For some reason he remembered what the property owner had said when he rented him the place. He had hoped that Danny wasn't superstitious. He said many people wouldn't take the place because of the number. Danny hadn't cared at the time, but today it seemed to mock him.

He threw his jacket across the dirty striped armchair he had rescued from the trash, and let his body fall down on the sagging couch.

"No place like home," he said aloud to himself. He felt utterly defeated. The woman who bailed him out of jail had used him for a patsy. He wasn't too smart but he could see that now.

The place was too quiet, except for the grandmother clock, a smaller version of the grandfather, that his mother left him when she died. It had been her mother's and she felt Danny should keep it. He hated the noisy thing, but it was all he had to remind of him of his family. He allowed himself to think about them. It was something he never dwelt on because it was too painful. Today he could think of nothing else. His father had been killed in a bar fight when he and his siblings were young. His brother had killed his sister, and almost killed him as well. His mother had always blamed his brother for killing the girl, and his brother finally committed suicide while he was still a young man. Even though he left no note, Danny knew it was because of the guilt. The family had never been close, and deep down he had always regretted it. Anyway, his mother had died only last year, leaving him nothing but the old clock: That loud ticking old clock. The deadly quiet of the apartment made it seem that much louder.

He hated the noisy families on the first and second floor, and he jumped at the chance when the landlord offered him the entire third floor to himself. Before, he had thought of it as being private, now it just seemed isolated.

Noise was what he needed. His feet echoed in the near empty rooms as he walked over and turned on the TV. The television blared to life, at first a flickering picture and then static. Taking his fist, he gave it a whack and the picture sprang back to life. There was nothing on but an infomercial, but at least it was company. Sitting down he leaned his head against the back of the couch. He was so tired. His roommate in jail had kept him awake all night raving and ranting about suing the damn cops. What he needed was a long nap. He would be able to think more clearly, after he slept.

Danny awoke with a start. The only light in the room was from the street outside. His forehead furrowed into a frown. Hadn't he left his lamp on? The television had been on, he was sure of that, but the only sound now was from the steady ticking of the grandmother clock. The sound was deafening in the room. He hoped his grandmother was happy about him keeping the thing, wherever she was. It was funny he should think of something like that.

The noise was just a tiny shuffle, some movement he couldn't account for. Had he locked his door? He couldn't remember. His eyes quickly searched the room and then he saw the figure. It was all dressed in black, standing on his right side a foot away from him. He started to get up, but he felt the cold steel of the gun barrel against his cheek. The killer was here and he was a dead man.

"Just sit still," the voice ordered. "We need to have a little talk."

"What do you want?" He could feel the cold sweat popping out on his face.

"I need to know how much you told Larkin," the woman hissed.

"I didn't tell him anything," Danny whimpered.

"You told him you didn't kill Julie Cromwell."

He heard the gun cock and he waited. Any minute now, his brains would splatter all over his apartment. "I-I didn't kill her."

Angrily she poked him with the gun. "You wouldn't have had to tell them anything if you'd stayed out of trouble like I told you."

"I told Larkin nothing. I don't even know who you are. How did you know where to find me?"

"I followed the cab here, dumb ass. You didn't even notice."

"I didn't tell Larkin anything. I told you, I don't know who you are."

The woman seemed to think about it a second. She moved in front of him and began to pace back and forth. "What exactly did you tell him?" She stopped, but in the dim light, he couldn't make out her face. Who was she? If someone planned to kill him, he had a right to know whom. He had to know her, if she knew him. He still didn't recognize her voice; of course, she might still be trying to disguise it.

His voice came out shrill. "They even made me take a polygraph. It proved that I don't know you."

"You idiot!" She caused him to jump when she yelled at him. "He knows if you didn't kill her, your accomplice did."

"He-he has no idea who you are."

"Larkin is smart. Don't you think he's figured it out?"

"Larkin is the one you need to kill, not me." Danny was used to talking his way out of situations like this. His size had made it necessary. "I can't hurt you. I don't know who you are." The truth was, he did know. He had figured out where he had heard the voice before, but the wasn't about to tell her. That wise-assed bitch had tried to tell him how to treat his own family. When he talked his way out of this, he was going straight to Larkin and ask for a deal.

"I'll kill you both. How's that?" She pointed the gun toward his head.

"I can't hurt you, Larkin can."

"You already have, you asshole. If you'd just kept it in your pants everything would have been okay. Men like you just can't do that, can you?" The anger churned her insides. She was a child again feeling the pain of a fourteen-year-old who the doctor has told she has lost her baby. Not only has she lost the child she wanted so badly, there would be no others.

In front of her, she saw the man who forced her into a sexual relationship she didn't want, one in which she was too young. He was the man who had ruined her life, so many years ago. She gritted her teeth and pulled the trigger.

The last thing Danny Preston heard was the shot, and that infernal clock kept ticking, and ticking.

Larkin heard the shots. He had just left the elevator when they sounded and he knew he was too late. He sprinted down the hall toward where the shots had come from. "Stop!" he yelled at the figure that had just burst through Danny's door. The figure raised their arm and shot. It felt like a sledgehammer hit him in the head, causing him to fall to the floor. The figure came toward him and bent over. He tried to focus his eyes, but because of the blinding pain, it was easier to let them close. Just when he expected the woman to put another bullet in him, he heard Cramer's voice calling him from the stairs. Then she was dragging him down the hall. He heard a door open and she rolled him inside. He heard her close the door and then he heard running footsteps as she scampered toward the back stairs.

Ted had just pressed the elevator button when he heard the shots. There was no time to wait: He sprinted up the stairs, two at a time. Maybe Larkin was right about him needing to lose a little weight, he decided. He was panting when he reached the top. Larkin was in trouble, he could feel it in his bones. His boss's car was outside in the front, and there was another vehicle also.

In front of him, he could see the elevator, to his left a hallway. He drew his gun, a .45 magnum, and keeping it in front of him he looked around. It was something he had learned from Larkin, to always be aware of his surroundings. There was a difference in the lighting from the first floor to the third. His eyes needed time to adjust, but there was no time. He began to move rapidly but cautiously down the hall, looking from left to right, afraid, my minute that someone would pop out of one of the rooms and blow him away.

Larkin had told him the apartment number, but he was having trouble seeing them in the dim lighting. Some of the numbers were gone, but there was enough left to know the uneven numbers were on the left. This ought to be the one he squinted to see. Standing to the side of the door, he turned the knob and waited to see if someone fired at him. He moved quickly into the room, his gun held in front of him, poised to shot anyone who tried to stop him. "Larkin, are you in here? It's Ted."

There was no answer. He could barely make out the bulk of the furniture. The heavy drapes shut out most of the light. Maybe there was a switch somewhere close to the door. He made his way forward, running his fingers along the wall praying he would find it. His fingers found the target, light flooded the room.

He could see an old chair with its back to him, and someone's head above the back of the chair. "Stand up and move away from the chair," he ordered.

The guy didn't move. Ted fired his gun into the ceiling. "I said to stand up."

There was no response.

Cramer moved like a cat, still holding his gun in front of him. He was in front of the seated man now. Ted swallowed. It was Danny

Preston, but he was not a threat. There was a hole in his head and blood was staining his shirt in the chest area. He moved quickly to Danny, taking his pulse, though he knew by the sightless eyes staring straight ahead that it was too late.

He had to find Larkin. He swallowed and made a quick scan of the room, telling him there was no one there except him and the corpse. "Larkin," he yelled again, but there was no sound except that damn clock. He wanted to shoot it, but he had to find his boss. His heart was thumping almost as loudly as the clock. He was afraid of finding Larkin in the same condition as Danny Preston.

Ted stepped into the hallway. That is when he saw the blood. It looked like someone dragged a wounded person down the hall. It stopped two rooms down from Danny's. He stepped to one side of the door and yelled, "It's the police, open up." He let the door swing open and could barely make out a crumpled body lying just beyond the door.

"Oh my God. Is that you, Larkin?" He bent over him, checking to see if he was breathing. A groan vibrated through the empty room, sending chills up Cramer's spine, but at least whoever it was, was still alive. He fumbled for the light switch, and turned it on.

Larkin began to come around. He had a graze wound to his forehead. Cramer ripped off his shirt trying to stop the flow of blood. He could hear the sirens from the backup he called arriving outside. Flipping open his phone he called an ambulance.

Larkin began trying to sit up. "Don't do that, man," Ted told him. "Just lay quietly until the medics get here."

"Did you get the license number?" Larkin mumbled.

"Carrie Risner's?" Ted asked impatiently. He couldn't believe the man might be dying and still worried about business.

"No; the Mack truck that hit me." He gave the other man a little half grin.

"No, I was too busy trying to save your butt from getting killed." Larkin had managed to roll up to a sitting position. "And I must say you did a good job too." Ted noticed that he was slurring his words.

Larkin was doing better before the paramedics arrived and Ted had told him about Danny Preston. They had determined that Carrie

Risner had fled down the back stairway when she heard Cramer calling to Larkin.

"How did you know it was Carrie Risner?" Larkin asked.

"I noticed the Porsche parked next to yours. I ran the plates, for I figured no one in this neighborhood would own a car like that. I also found out she was the one who house sat for the Davidsons."

Larkin tried to shake his head and almost passed out. "You're learning," Larkin said.

"I should say that my boss should take his own advice. Like waiting for backup."

"I was trying to save Danny Preston's life. And what's the deal about running plates before trying to save mine?"

Cramer Laughed. "I called it in out in the parking lot and they called me back while I was waiting for the elevator. This is an amazing tool." He held his cell phone out to Larkin. "No cop should be without one."

"It's made a believer out of me," Larkin agreed.

Larkin wanted to go with Ted and the others to pick Carrie up, but they insisted that he go to the hospital. Ted finally convinced him that he would have to get better so he would feel like interrogating her. He did want to be there. The woman was responsible for two murders and almost three.

Larkin gave Cramer a call from the hospital. The doctor had patched him up and he was feeling better.

"Did you pick her up yet?"

"Not exactly," Cramer said softly.

There was excessive noise all around him and Larkin could hardly hear.

"What's going on there?"

"I'm at the lake. Carrie Risner shot herself."

"She killed herself?"

"She put one through her brain."

"You're kidding." Larkin was shocked.

"I wish I was. The guys are wrapping up out here now, and I was just headed to let her family know. I hate this part of the job," Cramer said vehemently.

"Why don't you let me talk to her husband? I'm feeling much better now. At least I was until I heard this. But I don't understand. I thought you were going to her home. What was she doing at the lake?"

"Her husband called the station and told the officer on duty that she was on the way out there to kill herself. Mark called me on my cell phone."

"How did her husband know she was going there?"

"She left a note."

"The man must be crazy with worry," Larkin said. "I'm going out to the house."

"I don't think you should leave the hospital, let alone take care of something like this."

"I feel fine and if you like you can meet me there."

Cramer had been with him long enough to know it was useless to argue. At least he would be there in case he needed to go back to the hospital.

CHAPTER 23

———— ◆ ————

James Risner looked like hell. He welcomed Larkin and Cramer into his home as if he was glad to see a familiar face.

"Where is Toby?" Larkin didn't want to say anything in front of the boy.

"He's away at camp for a week. I thought about calling him, but I don't know what to say. He and his mother are so close." Deep sobs shook his body.

Larkin and Cramer waited for him to gain control, and then Larkin told him, "I see no need to call just yet. Not until you think of the right way to tell him."

James walked to a hall table and retrieved what looked to be a folded letter. "This is really to you, Mr. Larkin," he said, handing it to him.

Larkin took it and began to read aloud:

When you get this letter I will be dead. You will find my body at the lake. It's only fitting that I end it at the same place where I ended Julie's. I knew you had finally put it all together. The first thing I want you to know is that I never meant to kill you. If I had, you would be dead. I know you owe me nothing, but I'm begging you for a favor. Please make up a story about my death. I'm not asking because of myself, but for my husband and son. Don't ruin their lives because of what I did. I never wanted to get involved in the first place, but Julie insisted. She said she would tell my beautiful child that I wasn't his mother. I couldn't let her do that.

Yes, I hated her and yet I felt sorry for her. I knew what she had gone through. Both of us had our childhoods stolen from us by our own father. I don't know which of us he hurt the worst. All I know is that he ruined both of our lives

Larry was my boyfriend first, but once he saw my sister it was love at first sight. She didn't really want her second child and so she gave him to me. I was so desperate for a child I agreed to deceive Larry. We knew he would never give him up if he knew the child was his.

I tried to dissuade her when she got the fake kidnapping idea in her head. I tried to convince her she didn't need me to be involved. She said I knew all kinds of low lives because of my job and she wanted me to hire one. She said if I didn't go along with it, she would tell Toby that I wasn't his mother. The only person I could think of was Preston. He went along with it.

We were all supposed to meet at the lake; Preston and I would pick up our money and go on our merry way. She would wait a bit and then go on home. She was sure that her narrow escape would cause Larry to love her more.

I didn't go there to kill her. I took a gun with me, just in case something went wrong. I didn't trust Danny Preston. I was afraid he would try to keep all of the money, and since she railroaded me into this, I wanted the money for Toby. I figured he had a right to some of Larry's money.

I watched from the shadows while Preston picked up his share. He checked with a flashlight to see if the money was real and then he ran off into the night. I waited. I wanted to avoid a trap if the cops were involved. While I was watching, Julie took the other bag of money and brought it down on the dock. She stood there tapping her foot impatiently waiting for me to come. Anger began to boil up inside of me. I realized she had everything that I wanted and she was never satisfied. The only thing she did not have was Larry's son. It was just a matter of time before she tried to take him from me. She had already threatened to tell him the truth. I knew that she would use it against me as long as I lived. I decided to kill her right then.

When I stepped out of the shadows, the first thing she said was, 'Where have you been? I was about to throw your share of the money into the lake and go home.' She would have too. She was like that.

I hated that smug look on her face, so I blew her away. I threw the gun I had stolen from Cassie into the lake. Then I dumped her body also, took the money and went home.

When Cassie showed the gun to James I admired it. I heard her telling her dad that she kept it in her bedside table. I wanted the gun so one day I went to her place and waited for her to go. The door was unlocked so I went in and took it.

My husband knew nothing about any of this. He's a good man and I want him to know I tried hard to love him. By doing what I did, I am saving my husband and son the embarrassment of a long-drawn-out trail, and my going to prison.

To Toby and James, I say I am sorry, and ask them to forgive me. My sister and I were spawned in hell. Maybe now that we are both gone there will be a glimmer of hope for the next generation. I have tried to raise my son to be a good boy, and he is. Again, I say I am sorry.

PS. You will find the rest of the money in the attic. It is all there but what I used to bail Danny Preston out of jail.

"Wow!" Larkin said when he was finished. "This has got to be such a blow."

"I knew deep down that Toby belonged to Larry, but I never acknowledged it. I just wanted her to have some happiness in her Life."

Just then, the doorbell sounded and Lawrence Cromwell burst into the room. He went straight to James and caught him in a hug. Larkin motioned for Cramer and they prepared to leave. If anyone knew how James was feeling, it was Lawrence. Larkin could see him talking low to James and the other man nodding his head.

"We will finish this up tomorrow," Larkin called as he and Cramer left. James barely acknowledged the fact that they were leaving with a nod of his head.

"It's been a long day," Larkin said. "Why don't you head on home." The sun had long set and he was feeling the effects of what happened physically and mentally.

Instead of heading straight home, he wanted - no, needed - to see Cassie.

She ran to him as soon as he walked through her door. "Oh my God," Cassie exclaimed when she saw the patch covering one side of his head, almost obstructing the vision in his left eye. "My dad said you'd been hurt. He called me after he talked to Cramer," she explained.

"What did he tell you?"

"He said Carrie was the killer. He said she had killed Julie, and when you tried to arrest her, she shot you. I was so scared." She buried her head in his chest "You could have been killed."

"If Carrie had tried to kill me, I would be dead."

She pushed back so she could look at him. "You don't think she was trying to kill you?"

"No, I think she was trying to keep me from stopping her from doing what she had to do."

"You mean kill herself."

"Yes, that's exactly what I mean. I think she knew it was over, and she couldn't face bringing shame on her husband and son."

He held her for a time not saying anything, just softly caressing her back. She cried softly.

"Shush-" he consoled her. "It's all over."

She pushed away from him and told him, "It will never be over for our family, don't you understand? We will have to live with the scandals the rest of our lives. I don't really care about myself. I can take it. I hate it for my dad, and my brother and sister, and for poor James and Toby. What hell they must be going through." She went to the table and picked up a cigarette.

"I know..."

"No-you don't know, Larkin. My dad has asked me not to tell Todd and Tina they aren't his."

"That sounds like him," Larkin said.

"He has also decided not to tell Toby that he's his real dad. Do you know how that is eating him up inside?"

"I can only imagine."

"He has assured James that he won't try for custody of Toby." She faced Larkin to see what he thought about the idea. "You don't know how hard that was for him. He has always wanted a son and he knew Todd wasn't his."

"You said to me when we first met that your father was a good man. I reserved judgment at the time, but today I think that is an understatement."

"A few months ago my dad was interested in buying land for a strip mall. James Risner was going to do the construction. He has now changed his mind. He has purchased land on the outskirts of town and he and James are going to build a center for abused and neglected children. It will be in Carrie and Julie's honor and bear their names. I think it will be very good for both men, and this neighborhood."

"That is wonderful!" Larkin exclaimed. "I know I'll be sending him a lot of business."

Cassie smiled. "It seems they already have their first recruit. Do you remember Snake, Tina's boyfriend?

"Sure."

"James has offered him a job on weekends to help with the construction. The boy will now have regular meals and something to look forward to."

"Have you come to terms with your feelings for Julie?"

She thought about it for a second. "I do believe I am more tolerant. My dad knew that the woman he loved was suffering; I have to respect that. I can now see what the abuse has done to both she and Carrie. In time I think I will be able to forgive her."

"I'm glad to hear that."

"I've told my dad I will help him finish raising Todd and Tina. James has agreed to let us have a major part in Toby's life also."

Larkin smiled as he stared at her. "Your father has a pretty amazing daughter also."

"Let's face it. They couldn't help any of this. They're victims just Like the rest of us." She walked over to stand by the window. She was staring outside, but she seemed to be doing more thinking than seeing. "I'll drop the lease on my apartment, and my cat and I will be moving in with them. My dad has offered me the whole west wing. God knows the place is big enough for all of us."

"Cassie, I came here to offer you another proposition." He had come to her and put his arms around her once more. He turned her to face him.

"Don't say it, Larkin. I've thought long and hard about this and it just wouldn't work."

"We could make it work. I love you."

She put her finger to his lips to stop him. "I love you too, and I want to keep it that way. We would be at each other's throat in a week."

"We can both compromise."

"I'm a needy person, Larkin. I have baggage. I would have to have all your time and attention, and let's face it, you're married to your job."

"I'm willing to sacrifice."

"You're the crusader for justice, and you will push until you have done your job. The woman in your life will always have to take second place. That is all right because that is who you are. But I know myself, and that is not me." Her eyes pleaded with him to understand.

"Damn it, you're right. What the hell is wrong with me?"

She gently touched the side of his face. "There's nothing wrong with you. Besides my father, you're the greatest man I know."

"I will always love you," he choked past the lump in his throat.

"I feel the same."

"I don't suppose you would consider us seeing each other...?"

"I think you know me well enough to know, with me, it's all or nothing."

He hung his head and said, "I did know that."

She tiptoed up to kiss him. "Go get the bad guys, Larkin. I'll be rooting for you."

CHAPTER 24

———— ◆ ————

There was a subdued atmosphere around the office the next day. Larkin and Cramer were having coffee and discussing the tragedy of the Cromwell case when Mark, their favorite rookie, came into the office. "I want to congratulate you both on a job well done," he said with true admiration in his eyes. "I came to say that and to let you know that Mr. Deets wants to talk to Mr. Larkin, in his office..."

"Thanks, Mark," Cramer acknowledged. "Larkin and I were just discussing how we thought you might want to work with us on our next case."

"Could I? That is a dream come true."

"We'll see." Larkin smiled at the boy's enthusiasm. "Go tell Deets I'll be there in a minute."

"Yes, sir." The kid saluted before he left them.

"I wonder what he wants," Larkin said. "I'm having my coffee first. I don't think I can deal with him before caffeine."

"I'll be here in the office waiting for you," Cramer said. "If you need me, yell."

"Thanks, Cramer, for sticking with me through this."

"We're a team, man," he said, grabbing his boss in a bear hug. Then pushing away, he said, "Just don't go running off without backup, ever again."

"I've learned my lesson," he assured.

"Don't you take any crap from the gutless wonder," Cramer told him.

Larkin laughed. "I won't, but I may be fired when this is over." Seeing the worried look on Cramer's face, he told him, "I'll be fine."

"Come in," Deets answered Larkin's knock.

"You wanted to see me?"

"Have a seat," he offered, nervously shifting papers around on his desk. "How are you doing?" He noted the patch, which Larkin still wore. Larkin felt he asked for politeness' sake rather than concern.

"The wound is only superficial," he commented. It didn't hurt near as much as the searing pain in his heart.

"I'd rather stand if you don't mind. People have been insisting I sit down or lie down since this happened."

"Suit yourself," Deets said as he stood also. He was not a tall man. He wore built-up heels to make him look taller. It was a joke around the office. Maybe standing made him feel superior to his staff. He looked directly into Larkin's eyes as he spoke.

"I have to face a news broadcast in about thirty minutes." He consulted his watch.

"What does that have to do with me?"

"The news media wants you and Cramer there."

"Okay, I guess." There was a long pause, and Larkin asked, "Is there something else?"

"As a matter of fact there is."

Larkin sighed. It was always something with the man. "Well, what is it?"

"I really don't know how to say this."

"Just spit it out."

"This is the story that I am going to tell them, and you and Cramer are going along with it..."

"And what story is that?" Larkin could feel his hackles rising. He and the good DA had very different outlooks on most issues. He couldn't wait to hear Deets' take on this one.

"I will say that Danny Preston acted alone in the kidnapping and murder of Julie Cromwell. We mistakenly released him from jail. You went to his apartment to arrest him, he resisted, and he wounded you in the confrontation. You shot and killed him in self-defense." He drew in a breath, waiting for Larkin to go off. Larkin made no comment, and he continued, "Carrie Risner, upset by her sister's death, committed suicide."

"Okay," Larkin said simply, after Deets finished and breathed a sigh of relief.

Larkin didn't want the Cromwells' reputation dragged through the mud, any more than Deets did. The children's lives would be hell at school. Toby would suffer the most. Not only would he have to deal with his mother's death, but the fact that she killed her own sister. Danny had no family that would be hurt, except his wife and child, and there might be a way he could fix that.

"I know you think everything I do is because I'm a self-serving bastard, but damn it, Larry Cromwell is a good man and he has been through enough hell in his life. He deserves some peace. I can't see where telling the truth will do anyone any good."

"I agree."

"What?"

"I said, you're right."

Deets couldn't believe what he was hearing. He breathed another sigh of relief. He didn't believe that Larkin would go along with this without a fight.

Larkin was also thinking of Cassie. He wanted this to be as easy on her as he could make it.

"I do have one stipulation."

"What is that?" Deets seemed to hold his breath.

"Lawrence Cromwell offered a half-million-dollar reward to anyone who gave information leading to the killer."

"You don't mean you want the reward ... "

"Danny's wife actually told me where to find him. He had given her address as his and if it wasn't for her, I wouldn't have known where he was."

"I don't know..."

"I must tell you. Danny had an obsessive fear of guns and she knows it. If she talks to the media, she could cause us trouble. I suggest you get on the phone with Cromwell and explain the situation to him. You know that Dora Preston has no help supporting her daughter since Danny is gone. She will be upset about that."

"You're right. She could cause us trouble." The prosecutor's brow creased into a frown.

He didn't have to know that Danny never helped her in the first place. Larkin smiled. He had the man thinking.

"How do we know that this woman will go along with the story, even though we offer her the money? Some of these people are poor but proud." He made it sound obscene.

"Leave that to me," Larkin said.

"When you talk to Cromwell, tell him that Danny abused his wife and child and they really need a break."

Deets looked skeptical, but made no comment.

Larkin listened as Deets made the phone call to Larry, explaining the situation. He couldn't tell how things were going until he was off the phone.

"What did Larry say?" Deets' eyebrows rose at Larkin calling him by the shortened version of his name, but he made no comment.

"He said he didn't give a damn about the money, to give her what was left of the million."

It was hard for Larkin to contain himself. He wanted to shout and jump up and down. He almost high-fived the other man until he remembered it was Deets and not Cramer. Instead, he told Deets he would break the good news to Dora Preston.

Larkin heard Dora Preston go from devastated to the happiest woman in the world. She couldn't agree fast enough to go along with the story about Danny being the lone perpetrator of the crime. The only ones that would be hurt by the revelation would be her and her little girl, and with that kind of money they could change their names and move anywhere they wanted. She had been worrying about how she was going to come up with enough money to give Danny a decent funeral. Now she could do that. She owed him that much, at least. Asked if she would feel guilty about letting Danny take all of the blame, she assured Larkin she had no such feelings. If it were the other way around Danny would have done it in a heartbeat. She cried, and kept thanking Larkin for putting her in for the reward.

"It's show time," Larkin said as he hung up the phone. "She will go along with everything..."

Deets looked somewhat down. "What's the matter? You have hopes of using the money for your campaign?"

"It would have been nice." Deets stared at him a time before he spoke. "You know, Larkin, in your own way, you're as big a hustler as I am."

"What do you mean?"

"There is only one difference. Instead of feathering your own nest, you try to help all the Dora Prestons of the world. You will never be anything other than what you are right now, as long as you do that."

Larkin only smiled. How did you explain to someone like Deets that you didn't want to be anything else? You didn't, because people like him would never understand.

"Come on, Deets. The sharks are circling and we have a feeding frenzy to attend."

It was over. The media had their story. Cramer and the rest of the day shift had gone home. Larkin sat alone in his office waiting for the satisfaction that came from solving a difficult case. It would not come, for he felt that the real murderer had gotten off scot free.

Oh, he had tried his best to see that justice was done. He had gone all the way to Galvin to prosecute the man whom he considered responsible for the death of three of his children, only to find out that man had died quietly in his sleep. Another thing he wondered about was his wife. Did she go crazy before or after her children were abused, for years?

He learned from every case and this was no exception. He had realized that maybe his parents were not so bad after all. He had called them and he planned to try his hardest to reconcile before it was too late.

He also hoped that people like his parents and Linda Brown were right about there being an after life. He hoped if there was a hell that Nash Collins split it wide open. He also hoped it was extra hot.

Larkin was reminded once again, that justice is not always done, and the guy doesn't always get the girl, here in the real world.

CPSIA information can be obtained
at www.ICGtesting.com
Printed in the USA
BVHW031412300922
648383BV00009B/955

9 781959 165255